Whatever After

TWO PEAS in a POD

Read all the Whatever After books!

Whatever After

TWO PEAS in a POD

SARAH MLYNOWSKI

Scholastic Inc.

Copyright © 2018 by Sarah Mlynowski

This book was originally published in hardcover by Scholastic Press in 2018.

ISBN 978-1-338-16291-2

10 9 8 7 6 5 4 3 2 1   18 19 20 21 22

Printed in the U.S.A.   40

First printing 2018

for lauren walters:
royally awesome.

chapter one

Too Bad, So Sad

You know when you want something SOOO much and you're 99.9 percent sure you're going to get it? But there's a teensy chance you won't? (Only a very teensy chance.) And you can't eat or sleep or do anything but think about how excited you're going to be when you DO get it?

That's how I feel about getting picked to be student leader of our school carnival. Any second now, the principal is going to name the leader.

And it's going to be ME!

From my seat in the auditorium, I watch as Principal Braun

walks onto the stage. She taps the microphone. "Testing, one two," she says.

Ahhh! I can't take the suspense.

"And now," Ms. Braun continues, "I will announce who we have chosen to be the student leader of the carnival."

I sit up super straight in my chair. My best friend Frankie is sitting on my left side. Our other best friend, Robin, is on my right. The entire elementary school is here. Everyone is excited for the big announcement, but NO ONE is more excited than I am.

What does the student leader of the carnival do? So much! Like work with the teachers to plan all the activities, and help decide on fun games, yummy food, and awesome prizes.

I am very good at making decisions. For example, this morning, when my dad asked if I wanted pancakes or eggs, I immediately said pancakes — with blueberries. And yesterday, when my mom asked me which shoes went better with the black suit she was wearing for her big case — Mom's a lawyer, like Dad — I pointed to the red ones. Did my mom win her case with her red shoes? She totally did.

Did I mention I'm going to be a judge when I grow up? Because that's what judges do. Make decisions. Well, first I'm going to be a lawyer like my parents are, and then I'm going to be a judge because that's the way you have to do it. You also have to use a gavel. Okay, you probably don't *have* to use a gavel, but why would you not? Gavels are amazing.

Anyway.

Ms. Braun is fiddling with the microphone. She raises it slightly. This is it. The moment I've been waiting for. Earlier today, Ms. Braun and the teachers in charge of the carnival all got together to pick the student leader from the list of kids who applied.

Why am I so sure my name will be called?

First of all, to be the student leader, you have to be a fifth grader, the oldest grade in the school. And I am a fifth grader!

I know what you're thinking: *Big deal, Abby. There are A LOT of other fifth graders*. And you're right. But when the sign-up sheet was posted, I was the first person to put my name down. That shows just how much I want this.

Also, to apply for the position, you had to hand in five ideas for the carnival. And guess what? I came up with *ten*. Including a dunk tank, a booth where you can decorate your own cookies, and a booth where you can squeeze your own lemonade. Doesn't everyone want to squeeze their own lemonade? Yes. Of course! Everyone does!

The school carnival is supposedly the best part of Smithville Elementary. I missed last year's, since I didn't live in Smithville then, but everyone says it's incredible. It takes place over an entire Friday. And I'm going to lead it!

"It's definitely going to be you, Abby," Frankie whispers to me as she pushes her red glasses up on her nose.

I give her a grateful smile and shift in my seat nervously. To be on the safe side, I wore my lucky underwear today. Okay, fine, I don't really have lucky underwear, but these have green polka dots on them and green is a lucky color, so maybe they'll work.

"Definitely," Robin adds with such a serious nod that her reddish curls bounce on her shoulders.

"Or it will be someone else," Penny says from the other side of Robin.

Penny is Robin's *other* best friend. I glance over at her. She's examining her nails and looks totally bored.

Wow, THANKS, Penny. After everything we went through in Wonderland together? Where is the loyalty?

Ms. Braun clears her throat. "This year's leader of the school carnival is . . ."

I can't stop smiling! Should I stand up and wave to the crowd when my name is called? Yes, that seems like the right thing to do.

"Anisa Najeed!" Ms. Braun announces.

Yes! I stand up.

"Congrats, Anisa!" Ms. Braun adds.

Wait, what?

What did she just say?

Penny snort-laughs. "Sit down, Abby. She said Anisa Najeed."

The smile freezes on my face. My heart clenches. My stomach twists. I might cry. I need to sit. Yes, the first thing I need to do is sit.

I sit back down on the hard seat. Frankie puts her arm around me.

I can't believe it. I really thought I was going to get it. Did they actually pick Anisa? How is that possible?

There are loud noises all around me. Everyone is . . . clapping. Clapping?

Oh. They are clapping for Anisa.

Should I clap, too? Yes. I probably should. But I can't seem to do it.

"Rats," Frankie whispers. "I'm sorry, Abby. I know how badly you wanted to win."

Robin makes a sad face. "You can have the brownie my mom packed me for dessert at lunch," she says.

"Thanks, guys," I barely manage to croak out.

I try to look like I'm not upset. But how do you make your eyes un-teary, your face un-splotchy, and your expression un-miserable when you're ready to sob like a toddler who just dropped her ice cream cone on the floor?

How could the teachers choose Anisa instead of me? She barely talks. Yesterday, she was sitting at our lunch table and I didn't even realize she was there. Because she didn't say one word the whole time! How can someone be a leader if she's as quiet as a pet turtle? It's going to be a horrible carnival.

We're dismissed from the auditorium and I walk out into the hallway with Robin, Frankie, and Penny. Everyone is swarming around Anisa, congratulating her. I feel myself starting to get mad. This is totally unfair.

Uh-oh. Oh, no. Anisa is looking at me. She's tilting her head. She's biting her lower lip.

She's walking toward me.

Crumbs.

"Hi, Abby," Anisa says to me. She is pretty, with long black hair, brown skin, and dark brown eyes.

I know I'm supposed to congratulate her. But all that comes out of my mouth is "Hi."

She's not saying anything else, either. Because she's TOO QUIET.

We stare at each other. AWK-WARD.

"Um, Abby?" she says.

"Yeah?" I ask. I cross my arms in front of my chest.

"Will you help me with the carnival?" Anisa asks. "I know you have some great ideas."

I can feel my cheeks burning. My face must be bright red.

She wants *me* to be *her* second-in-command? No way.

"Uh, sorry," I mumble. "I'm, um, really busy. Super busy. I have a lot of homework and I have a dog and a brother and they both need me to, um . . . spend time with them. And stuff."

Anisa gives me a confused smile. Luckily, a bunch of other kids surround her to congratulate her, and I slip away.

"So annoying," I whisper to Frankie and Robin, rejoining them.

"Too bad, so sad," Penny says, flipping her blond hair behind her shoulder. "But honestly, Abby, who cares?" She leans close to me and whispers, "You have much cooler things in your life than an elementary school carnival."

"Shhhhh," I whisper back. Am I going to have to spend my entire life worrying that Penny is going to give away my secret?

I think I am.

Here's what Penny is referring to: I have a magic mirror in the basement of my house. I really do. My little brother, Jonah, and I discovered it when we moved to Smithville. If you knock on the mirror three times at midnight, a magic fairy turns the mirror into a portal that takes you into different fairy tales. It sounds like I'm joking, but I'm not. I've visited fairy tales like *The Frog Prince* and *Cinderella* and *Hansel and Gretel*. And yeah. The witch in that one totally tried to eat us. But snacking on her candy house made it almost worth it.

Usually, just my brother and I (and our dog, Prince) go into the fairy tales. Robin came into *Sleeping Beauty* with me, but she pricked her finger and fell asleep and doesn't remember. But a couple of weeks ago, Penny, Frankie, Robin, and I went through a *different* portal (in a golf course) and ended up going into Wonderland. As in *Alice's Adventures in Wonderland*.

Frankie and Robin don't remember being in Wonderland because they were sprinkled with magic powder. But Penny wasn't sprinkled with much of it, so she remembers everything. Part of me hates that Penny knows I go into stories — her of all people! But part of me kind of likes that at least somebody, even Penny, knows my secret.

She's asked me if she can sleep over five times in the last two weeks. She desperately wants to go to fairy tale land.

Still, even having this cool magical secret can't cheer me up today. Ahead of us in the hallway, more kids are crowding around the new carnival leader.

"Yay, Anisa!" a fourth-grade girl cheers. "Can't wait for the carnival! You're going to have a cotton candy machine, right?"

"Yup," Anisa says. "Blue and pink."

I scowl. Blue and pink? Seriously? She should obviously have the cotton candy in our school colors. Blue and *yellow.* But I'm not going to suggest that. Nope. I am done giving away my carnival ideas. They don't want me to be in charge? Then they don't get my ideas.

Too bad, so sad.

chapter two

Rain, Rain, Go Away

O kay, let's go," my brother, Jonah, says that night, waking me from a restless sleep.

I scowl and open my eyes. Jonah is standing in my room, right by my bed. Our dog, Prince, an adorable brown-and-white mutt, is next to Jonah, wagging his tail.

I glance at my alarm clock. It's 11:45 P.M. Jonah is only seven, and his bedtime was HOURS ago.

He's wearing a green hoodie. And his sneakers.

He's dressed to go somewhere. At close to midnight.

I know what he's trying to do.

Ever since I got home from school, everyone has been trying to make me feel better about not being chosen as the leader of the carnival. Nothing has worked. Not one of my favorite dinners — spaghetti and meatballs. Not family movie night. Not even phone calls from both Frankie and Robin making sure I'm okay.

(I said I am, but I'm not.)

"I don't feel like going into a fairy tale," I tell Jonah now. "Forget it." I pull my blanket over my head.

"But, Ab-by," Jonah singsongs. "Guess what I have. M&M's. And I saved you all the blue ones, your favorite."

I throw the blanket off my head and sit up. I hold out my hand.

Jonah grins and sits down next to me. He reaches into his pocket and pulls out five mashed-up, cracked blue M&M's. He pours them in my palm. They're hot. So gross.

But they're M&M's, so I pop the handful in my mouth anyway. But not even candy can make me happy. "I'm too upset to go," I tell him.

"Come on, Abby!" Jonah says. "It'll take your mind off not getting picked."

"It's hopeless. Go back to bed." I flop down and pull the covers over my head again.

Prince jumps up on my bed. He grabs the edge of my blanket with his teeth and pulls it back.

I hear Jonah laugh.

"Prince! Go away," I say.

Prince does not go away. He nudges my shoulder with his little chocolate-colored nose.

"C'mon, Abby," Jonah says. "We gotta move. It's almost midnight."

"No."

Woof! Prince whisper-barks, as if he's suddenly had an idea. Then he hops off my bed and takes off running out of my room.

We hear him scurrying down the stairs.

Uh-oh.

"Now you don't have a choice," Jonah says gleefully. "You know Prince will go without us!"

Ahhh! Prince totally will. All he has to do is hit the mirror three times with his paw to make it swirl. He's done it before.

I want to pull the blankets back over my head, but I can't. I *have* to stop Prince.

I jump out of bed, slip on my sneakers, and pick up my orange-and-white watch from my desk. My watch keeps track of the time back home, and if we end up in a fairy tale, I'll need it to know what time it is here.

Jonah and I hurry down the stairs, trying to be quiet. My parents don't know about the magic mirror — and can't know. We round the curve and go down the steps to the basement. Prince is standing right in front of the mirror, waiting patiently. Aw, good boy.

The mirror is huge — twice the size of me — and has a stone frame decorated with fairies and wands. Prince lets out a small *woof* and presses on the glass part of the mirror with his paw.

"Prince, no!" I whisper-shout.

The mirror starts to hiss.

Hmm. That means that Maryrose — the fairy who's cursed to live inside our mirror — is going to let us go through. She doesn't always. Sometimes we knock and knock and nothing happens.

Does she know what happened at school today? She does seem to know everything. Except how to get herself un-cursed.

I keep trying to help her with that. Unsuccessfully. Which isn't that surprising, considering I can't even get myself chosen as leader of the school carnival.

I'm feeling very sorry for myself, thank you very much.

"Enough, Prince," I say, trying to grab his collar and pull him away.

But Prince wiggles out of my grasp and nudges the mirror again. He is not the best listener. He has a lot of puppy in him.

The mirror turns purple.

Oh, great. We're almost at the place of no return! Although . . . If Maryrose is letting us in, then that means she *wants* us to go in. Maybe she has a mission for us.

Prince leaps at the mirror with his paw. I don't stop him this time.

The mirror starts swirling.

Should I go? Yes. No. I don't know!

"Prince, wait!" I say.

Prince eyes me. He doesn't move.

"Prince, jump through!" Jonah says.

My mouth drops open.

And Prince leaps right into the mirror, through the swirling purple portal. And then he's gone.

"Jonaaaaaaah!" I cry. "Why did you do that? I was still debating! Now we have no choice!"

My brother gives me a sheepish grin. "Right! We have no choice! See you in the fairy tale!" He waves and jumps inside.

WHAT? Did my little brother and Prince just go through on their own?

AHHH!

I can't see Prince or Jonah. All I see is swirling purple.

Obviously, I can't let them land in some fairy tale without me.

"I'm coming, Jonah!" I cry, and leap through.

I land on my butt. Ouch.

It's hot here. And humid. Steamy. It feels like the sauna that my mom once took me to when we were at a spa in a hotel.

The air smells good, fresh, like palm trees and flowers. It's dark, so it must be nighttime here.

"Jonah?" I call. "Prince?"

A raindrop lands on my head. Oh, no. Of course I have no umbrella.

Another raindrop. And another. And then — whoosh! The rain goes from drizzling to downpour in seconds. My flannel pajamas are soaked.

Oh, crumbs, I'm wearing flannel pajamas. I wasn't supposed

to go into a fairy tale tonight! I was supposed to sulk about my sad situation!

And where are Jonah and Prince? I swivel my head and squint in the dark, trying to see through the sheets of rain.

Wait — something is glinting. It's the silver buckle of Prince's collar. Yes, there he is! He's getting as soaked as I am. And there, sitting right next to Prince, is a very wet Jonah. Whew.

"Abby!" Jonah says, jumping to his feet and racing over to me. Prince bounds over, too. "I knew you'd come. Are you feeling better now?"

"Because getting rained on is fun?" I ask, getting to my feet.

"No, because going into stories is fun."

True. It is.

The rain is not letting up. Jonah pulls his hoodie tighter around his head. I really wish I wasn't wearing wet flannel. Prince shakes his fur.

"Well," Jonah says, "it might be dark and raining, but at least you won't be thinking about the carnival."

"Why not?" I ask.

"Because you'll be too busy figuring out where we are, what

we have to do, and how to get home," Jonah says, cocking his head to the side.

Jonah's right. I *am* distracted by our new surroundings. But the carnival is still in the back of my mind. Annoying me. Like a teeny, tiny splinter in my brain.

I glance around. My eyes are adjusting to the dark, and I can see lush greenery and palm fronds, which look like fans. Could we be in a jungle? On an island?

"Let's walk until we come to something we recognize," I suggest. "Then we'll know what story we're in."

"Look," Jonah says, pointing. "There's a path through the grass. Should we follow it?"

"Might as well," I say.

As we walk, Jonah keeps craning his neck and looking up at the sky.

"Uh, Jonah? First of all, watch where you're going or you're going to trip," I say. "Second of all, what are you looking for?"

"A beanstalk," he says.

I roll my eyes. Of course he is. My little brother is OBSESSED with *Jack and the Beanstalk*. We haven't gone into that fairy tale yet, but he is always hoping we will.

"Well, I don't see a farm or a cow or a beanstalk or a giant," I say. "But let's keep walking."

Jonah's face brightens. Prince scampers ahead of us. The rain has let up and now it's just very warm and humid.

Jonah reaches into his hoodie pocket and pops an M&M into his mouth. "Want one?" he asks. "You already ate all the blue ones. I only have a few left."

"Let's not waste them," I say. "We might be starving in a few hours."

I spot a muddy body of water to our left. There are toads, lizards, and weird-looking insects crawling all over the low green bushes beside it.

Eek.

"I think that's a swamp," I tell Jonah.

"What's a swamp?" Jonah asks.

I try to remember what we learned about swamps at school. "I'm pretty sure they're flooded areas of land. And when rivers and lakes overflow from rain, you get a swamp."

Jonah's shoulders slump. "I'm guessing there are no swamps in *Jack and the Beanstalk*?"

"I don't think so," I say. "Sorry."

Jonah kicks at a pebble. "But at least now I know what story we ARE in."

I raise an eyebrow. How could he know?

"Which one?" I ask.

"The one that has a swamp in it!" he says, and looks very pleased with himself.

"Oh, THAT one," I say with a laugh, and shake my head. Little brothers.

I try to remember all the fairy tales my nana read us before we moved to Smithville. "I can't think of any fairy tales with a swamp."

Jonah scrunches up his face. He looks like he's about to suggest something — probably *Jack and the Beanstalk* again — when we hear Prince let out a weird, low growl. He's come to a stop ahead of us, his ears pricked up and his little body tense.

Grr-woof! Grr-woof! Our dog is growling at something near the swamp's edge.

"What's wrong, Prince?" Jonah asks, taking a step closer to the swamp.

Growl-woof! Growl-woof! Prince barks again.

And then Prince does something really strange. He slinks down like he's afraid, and lets out a whine.

Jonah and I stare at each other.

What. Is. Out. There???

And then I see it.

Big. Yellow. Eyes.

Pointy. White. Teeth.

A super-long, super-big slithering green body.

"ALLIGATOR!" I shout at the top of my lungs.

YEP. Just a few feet away, coming out of the swamp onto the grass, is a massive green alligator.

AHHHH!

Why are we standing here waiting for it to eat us?

"Run, Jonah," I cry. "Run!"

chapter three

Milk and Cookies

Jonah and I take off, with Prince right on our heels, whimpering and barking.

We run through puddles, following the path. My heart is racing. "Are alligators fast?" I ask. "Probably not, right? Because they have such small feet?"

"Actually," Jonah says, "they can run like thirty miles an hour! I read a book about them!"

Great. Just great.

I dare a look behind us as we keep running. I don't spot the gator, but that doesn't mean it's not slithering along the high grass, hungry and waiting to eat us.

Jonah is breathing hard as he runs next to me. "Hey, Abby —
is that a light up ahead?" he pants.

I have no idea because I've been running with my head
turned back, looking for the gator.

But when I glance in front of me, I see there is a light, the
kind that comes from a window where someone is awake.
Hopefully, a non-alligator someone.

"Let's go, let's go!" I cry.

A castle comes into view. It's huge and made of stone and has
a bunch of turrets. The light seems to be coming from one of its
many windows. A moat surrounds the castle, and I can see that
the moat is connected to the swamp.

I have no clue what story we're in. Or who lives in this
castle.

What I DO know? That a humongous alligator is hot on our
tail. So best to keep going.

Jonah, Prince, and I race across a short drawbridge over the
moat, to the castle's arched entrance. I raise my hand and pound
on the door. Another light comes on inside. I hear footsteps. I
hear someone unlocking the door.

In the real world, I would never knock on a strange door in

the middle of the night. But what choice do I have? There's an alligator after me!

I hold my breath as the door opens.

The girl standing there is wearing a green dress and a white apron. She has shoulder-length straight brown hair, brown eyes, and a few freckles across her nose. I think she's a couple of years older than I am.

She doesn't say anything.

Is she waiting for me to speak?

Um, probably. I *am* the stranger at the door.

"Hi!" I rush to say. "I'm Abby and this is my brother, Jonah, and that's our dog, Prince. Can we come in? We're lost and soaking wet and we're being chased by a giant alligator!"

She bites her lip and says something so quietly that I can't hear her.

"Excuse me?" I ask her, leaning closer while glancing all around to make sure the alligator isn't behind us. I don't see it. For now.

"Come in," the girl says, a bit louder, opening the door wider.

Whew.

We hurry in and she shuts the door. For a moment, I'm so

relieved that I forget everything else. Like being in a castle with who knows who, who knows where, about to face who knows what.

"Please wait here," the girl says. "I'll be right back."

At least that's what I think she says. She half mumbled it and was looking down as she said it.

I watch the girl dart down the hall, knock on a door, and go inside.

It's much cooler in here, which is nice after the humidity. I take a look around. The castle's decor is very modern, with white leather couches and a pink-and-purple rug. Ooh — there's a clock on the wall. It's one A.M. I glance down at my wrist. According to my watch, the time at home is 12:06 A.M.

It feels like at least an hour has passed since we went through the mirror. Does that mean that every minute at home is ten minutes here? I'll have to keep an eye on the clock and on my watch to make sure.

"Do you think that girl went to get the royals who live here?" Jonah asks me.

"Maybe," I say. Prince has wandered over to the rug and is starting to gnaw on its tassel. I stop him.

"Um, Abby?" Jonah adds. "No offense but . . ."

I narrow my eyes at my brother. "But what?"

Jonah is trying to keep himself from bursting out laughing. "You should really fix your hair if we're about to meet a princess. You look like you stuck your finger in an electric socket."

I reach up to touch my curly brown hair. It's gotten huge and puffy from the humidity. It must be a frizzy mess.

"You should see yours," I say, nodding toward the giant curly mop on my brother's head.

Jonah grins. "We look like swamp creatures!"

Before I can try to find a mirror and fix my hair, the door down the hall opens. An older man and woman, both around my nana's age, come out. The girl who let us in is behind them.

"Hello, children!" the woman says. She has black-gray hair pulled back into a bun, dark skin, and warm brown eyes. She's wearing a long, green velvet bathrobe, and a pair of fur slippers. "My name is Minerva and this is my husband, Lawrence."

Lawrence gives us a big smile. He's short and has thick silver hair and dark skin. He's wearing the same kind of bathrobe as his wife, long and green, and the same fur slippers. "It's a pleasure to meet you," Lawrence says. "Belly here says you got lost and that an alligator was after you?"

Belly? I glance behind Lawrence and Minerva. The girl who let us in is biting her lip again and looks at the ground.

25

"Belly is one of the castle's best maids," Minerva says, patting the girl on the shoulder. "Belly, why don't you go to the kitchen and fetch a snack for our guests."

"And two of our fluffiest towels," Lawrence adds. "Abby and Jonah look soaked to the bone."

"We are!" Jonah says. "If I shake my head, I could spray you like Prince does after we give him a bath."

Minerva and Lawrence laugh like that's the funniest thing they've ever heard. They seem truly happy that we're here. Maybe they don't get a lot of guests? Or maybe the alligator eats most of the would-be visitors before they can ever make it to the castle.

"And you, Abby? Are you feeling frail at all?" Minerva asks me intently.

Frail? I shrug. I guess I am a little shaken up from that alligator chase. And wet from the rain.

"It would be nice to dry off," I say.

Lawrence and Minerva smile at me. They're smiling as if I've done something amazing like bake a cake or cure cancer.

Not that baking a cake is as impressive as curing cancer. Obviously.

I smile back and then glance away. When I look at them again, they're still smiling — and staring.

Not at Jonah. Not at Prince.

At me.

They start whispering to each other. Lawrence points at me. Minerva nods.

More whispering. More smiling and staring.

Is it the giant frizz puff on my head?

"They're being weird," I whisper to Jonah.

Woof, Prince barks, clearly in agreement.

I'm about to ask Lawrence and Minerva — politely — what they're talking about, when Belly returns. She's wheeling a cart that contains a tray of cookies, a pitcher of milk, two cups, and a stack of thick towels.

Belly drapes a warm towel around me and then one around Jonah. I use the edge to dry my face. Ahhh. That feels good. And I *do* like cookies . . .

"Are those chocolate chip?" Jonah says, eyeing the tray. "Please tell me they're not raisin cookies."

"Yes! Chocolate chip!" Minerva says with a grin. "We have a wonderful baker. Enjoy your snack, children. And when you're done, I'll show you to your room. I assume you need a place to stay for the night?"

"Belly, please go set up their room," Lawrence adds.

Minerva whispers something to Belly, who nods, glances at me, and scurries away.

Weird.

"Abby, can we stay?" Jonah asks me, his mouth already full of chocolate-chip cookie. "I'm really tired. Pretty please?"

Hmmm. I'm tired, too. And Lawrence and Minerva seem very kind. But I'd like to know more about where we are, to make sure this is a safe place for us.

"Is this your castle?" I ask, reaching for a cookie and taking a bite. Mmmm. Incredibly good. I devour the cookie and pour myself a glass of milk. Yum. So cold and delicious. Jonah has already scarfed down *three* cookies and has a milk mustache. I give him a nudge and he licks it away.

"Does Jack live here?" Jonah asks hopefully.

I swallow a laugh.

"Jack?" Minerva repeats. "Who's Jack? Only Lawrence and I live here with the castle staff."

"Are you the king and queen?" Jonah asks, biting into a fourth cookie. He uses his towel to wipe off the crumbs.

"Oh, goodness, no," Lawrence says. "Sadly, the king passed away recently. And the queen died many years ago. I was the king's advisor."

"What does an advisor do?" Jonah asks, sipping more milk.

"It was my job to help the king make important decisions about the kingdom of Bog," Lawrence explains, which reminds me of the carnival for a moment. I push the thought away.

"Bog?" I repeat.

Lawrence smiles. "Yes. Bog. As in, a flooded area. There are many swamps and rivers here, and the ocean is off on the far side of the kingdom. With all the rain, the bodies of water flood often. Brings out the gators."

There's more than one?

I swallow hard.

"We don't have to go back out there, do we, Abby?" Jonah asks, glancing out the window.

"We do have a very comfortable room for you," Minerva pipes up, "with a closet full of dry clothes."

Dry clothes sound amazing right now. Do we have enough time to stay overnight, though? We have to be back in Smithville by seven A.M. so our parents find us in our beds.

I look at my watch again. It says 12:07 now. Then I look up at the clock on the wall. It's now 1:10. So yes — every minute at home is ten minutes here. Every hour at home is ten hours here. Which means we can stay here for almost three days.

Plenty of time NOT to think about the carnival back home.

Prince lets out a bark, and Lawrence smiles down at him.

"If you stay," Lawrence tells us, "we'll make sure that Belly puts aside a bone for your dog's breakfast in the morning."

Aw, that's thoughtful.

"All right," I say to our hosts. "We'll stay. Thank you for your hospitality."

"Fantastic!" Minerva exclaims. "Follow me."

"I will see you in the morning, children," Lawrence says, turning to go. "Good night."

"Good night!" Jonah says. "Thanks for the snack! And thank the baker for not making raisin cookies."

Lawrence laughs and heads back into his room. Minerva starts leading us up the grand staircase. "C'mon, Prince," I say, and he follows behind.

There are many doors on the second floor, but only one with pink-and-purple stripes on it. That's the one Minerva opens.

"Here you are, children," Minerva says. "You'll find paja-mas in the bottom drawer of the dressers."

We step inside and I gasp.

Smack in the middle of the very fancy room are two beds. Two GIANT beds. Each one has a ton of mattresses piled on top. Like a hundred. I very quickly count by twos. There ARE a hundred mattresses exactly! On each bed! Way up top I see a pink quilt and fluffy pillows.

Jonah won't have any trouble climbing up *his* mattresses — he's a champion climber. But how am I supposed to get up to the top of my bed?

I freeze.

Wait a minute. Hold up.

A castle. A bed with one hundred mattresses.

OMG!

We're in *The Princess and the Pea*!

chapter four

Ninety-Nine, One Hundred

I wait until Minerva has wished us good night and left the room before I turn to Jonah.

"I know what fairy tale we're in!" I exclaim. "Don't you?"

Jonah shakes his head. I roll my eyes.

"Don't you remember Nana reading us *The Princess and the Pea*?" I ask.

Jonah wrinkles his nose. "I hate peas. They're mushy."

"I totally agree. But according to the story, a real princess is able to feel a pea that's under the bottom mattress even though there are a ton of mattresses piled on top of it."

Jonah scrunches up his face. "How is that possible? It

would be totally squashed. Unless it's a frozen pea. Is it a frozen pea?"

"I don't know. Probably not. But in the story, a girl claiming to be a princess felt the pea. And that's how everyone knew she was truly a princess."

"But why would anyone care if she could feel a pea?" Jonah argues. "I sat on a string bean at dinner last night and didn't even say anything. I just peeled it off my pants."

I laugh. "Should I tell you the whole story?"

"Yes, peas."

"Okay. So a prince wanted to marry a princess — but only a real princess. And he couldn't find one. One rainy night, a girl came to his castle, seeking shelter from the storm. She claimed to be a princess."

"Was she?" Jonah asks.

"Well, his mother, the queen, wasn't sure. So she decided to make the girl prove it."

"So the queen put a pea under the girl's mattress to see if she could feel it?" Jonah asks.

"The queen put the pea under the FIRST mattress — and then a whole bunch more mattresses on top. Only a real princess would be able to feel the tiny pea under all those mattresses."

"So in the morning, the girl said the bed was really uncomfortable?" Jonah asks.

"Yup. She couldn't sleep a wink. So they knew."

"And the prince found his princess," Jonah says.

"Right."

"Did the princess eat the pea for breakfast the next morning?" Jonah asks.

"I doubt it," I say. "That's kind of disgusting."

He smiles. "Not if it had ketchup on it."

I sigh. My brother is obsessed with ketchup.

There's a knock on the door, and Belly pokes her head in the room.

"It's me, Belly. I've brought your ladders for you," she says shyly.

Ladders. Of course. *That's* how I'll be able to get up to the top of the bed.

"Thanks," I say as Belly comes inside holding two ladders.

"I like your name," Jonah tells her.

Belly smiles. "My real name is Isabelle, but everyone calls me Belly for short." She places a ladder at the end of each bed.

"So, Belly," I say. "Will we meet the prince in the morning?"

She looks at me in total confusion. "What prince?"

"Doesn't a prince live here?" I ask. I mean, isn't that why they have the mattresses set up like this? Just in case they have to test a princess?

"No prince lives here," she says.

"Why are there beds with a hundred mattresses?" Jonah asks. "I mean, why not just one mattress per bed? Isn't that the normal way?"

My questions exactly. Thank you, Jonah.

Belly bites her lip. "Tradition, I guess."

"Tradition?" I ask.

"Because there's so much flooding here in Bog," Belly says. "If you're up high, you won't get wet. We give guests extra mattresses just in case. Bog is actually famous for its mattresses. Back when our dear departed king was young, he started a mattress factory. There are several mattress stores in the village. Even the people from the neighboring kingdom of Bug come here to buy their mattresses because the quality is so good."

Jonah's eyes practically pop out of his head. "Did you say BUG?"

Belly giggles. "Yes. Bug. It used to have a different name, but got renamed for how buggy it became. Here in Bog, we have such a big alligator population that the baby alligators eat most of the insects. But over in Bug, the villagers are constantly getting bitten now. They go through a lot of insect repellent."

"Why doesn't Bug have alligators?" I ask. "Don't alligators just slither around any swamps they want?"

"Yes," Belly says. "But here in Bog we understand that we must share our land, and our swamps, with swamp creatures. We're respectful of all nature, including the gators. Prince Micha of Bug HATES alligators and tries to catch them. Even the baby gators! He even poisoned some of them! So all the swamp creatures that were in Bug's swamps left and now live in our swamps."

Oh, great. Double the alligators. Thanks, Prince Micha.

"Well, I'll let you two settle in," Belly says, heading for the door. "I'll be back to check on you in a bit."

When the door closes behind Belly, I go over to the white dresser against the wall and open the bottom drawer. Lots of pajamas. I take out a pair of footed purple striped ones for myself and hand Jonah footed robot pj's.

There's an amazing bathroom attached to our room with a pink-and-purple spa tub, and after we each change and wash up, Jonah and I are both yawning and ready for bed.

Jonah scurries up his ladder in two seconds. My brother is definitely part monkey.

I watch as he cannonballs into the center of the top mattress.

"Wheeee! This is fun!" He lands on his stomach. "So comfortable. I should ask Mom and Dad to get me a hundred mattresses at home."

Prince barks like crazy from the floor.

"Oops, forgot you!" Jonah says. He climbs back down, picks up Prince, climbs back up, and puts Prince on the bed.

Prince wags his tail happily and starts sniffing the edge of the mattress.

Yikes.

"Careful, Prince," I say.

Prince keeps sniffing. And then he rolls right off the bed.

"Prince!" I yell as he tumbles through the air.

Incredibly, he lands on all four paws. He looks stunned but right away starts whining for Jonah to take him to the top again.

I guess my dog is part monkey, too.

I take a deep breath and stare up, up, up, at my one hundred mattresses.

Am I really supposed to sleep all the way up there? What if I fall off? What if I'm flipping onto my stomach and miss the edge of the bed by an inch and then roll off and break my neck? I'm zero percent monkey.

"Abby!"

I peer up. Jonah's face is hanging over the top of his top mattress. "Go up! It's so comfy!"

I put my foot on the ladder. Seems steady, I guess. I climb up. Carefully. Carefully. Ninety-eight mattresses, ninety-nine, one hundred. Whew. I make it to the top mattress and sit down on it hesitantly.

"Night, Abby," Jonah says. He pulls his quilt up, fluffs his pillow, and starts snoring. Prince curls up beside him and starts snoring, too.

I lie down on the soft pillow and pull the quilt up to my neck. I really am tired.

I close my eyes.

I won't roll off the top mattress. I won't.

I open my eyes.

But what if I do?

Well, I definitely won't roll off if I'm on my stomach. I very, very carefully flip over.

But why doesn't this bed have rails on the sides? It's kinda dangerous. And they could have put the bed against the wall. At least one side would have been safe.

I flick my eyes from side to side.

I can't sleep on here. I just can't. It's too dangerous! Maybe I can knock the top mattress off onto the floor and just sleep on that. I try to pull it a bit, but I can't budge it while I'm on it.

That's it — I'm getting off this thing. I'll sleep on the rug. At least I won't fall to my death in the middle of the night.

I reach for the ladder. But it's . . . gone?

Ahhh! Where's the ladder?

Belly must have come back to check on us, thought we were asleep, and took the ladders away until morning.

I'm trapped up here! I can't get down!

What if I have to go to the bathroom?

I have to go to the bathroom.

No, I don't. But I might. And what then?

"Jonah?" I call, hopeful when he turns his head. But he's fast asleep, his mouth open.

Great. Just great.

I very, very carefully flip over to my back and stare at the ceiling.

This is going to be a long night.

chapter five

Up All Night

La, la, la. The sun is up, the sun is up! I am delirious with exhaustion! I haven't slept at all! I haven't moved in seven hours! I am very tired! Very, very tired!

My brother is still fast asleep.

"Jonah!" I call to him.

He doesn't even stir.

"Jonah!" I yell louder.

He opens one eye. Prince gets up, stretches, then *leaps* over onto my bed.

"Careful!" I call to Prince.

He licks my cheek.

Jonah sits up and stretches. He's smiling. Smiling! As though everything is normal! As if I didn't just spend the entire night staring at the ceiling!

"Good morning," my brother says. "I had the best night's sleep of my life. I really wish I could have a hundred mattresses at home. Maybe I'll ask for them for my birthday?"

"No," I say. "No, no, no. How did you sleep so well? Weren't you afraid of falling off?"

"Why would I fall off?" he asks.

"Because we're up so high!"

"But, Abbs, that makes no sense. I'm not more likely to fall off here just because it's high. And it's not like I fall off at home. Why would I fall off here?"

Oh. Right. That is a very good point. Why didn't I think about that last night?!

There's a knock at the door. "Come in," I say. Please be Belly with that ladder! GET ME OFF THIS THING.

Belly pokes her head in. Her brown hair is in a tiny bun. "Good morning," she says with a smile. "I brought the ladders back."

"Why didn't you just leave them where they were?" I ask.

"It's tradition to remove the ladder," she says.

Tradition is big here. Fear of heights is not.

41

"Minerva and Lawrence would like you to join them for breakfast in half an hour," she says. Then she stares at me before leaving.

"Jonah, did you notice her staring at me?" I ask.

Jonah looks at me. "Well, you do look a little . . . deranged."

"Excuse me?"

"Your hair is all over the place, and your eyes kind of look like Slinkys. Like they're going to pop out of your eye sockets."

"Gee, thanks."

"You look tired," he clarifies.

"I AM tired!" I say as I climb down the ladder. I've never been so thrilled to see a ladder in my life. Hello, ladder. I love you, ladder.

Once on the floor, I stretch. Ah. That feels good.

Jonah and I take turns using the bathroom. We should probably change our clothes for breakfast, but I don't want to borrow any outfits without asking. So we go out into the hallway with Prince, wearing our pajamas. Belly is sitting on a chair outside, reading a book called *Swamplands: The History of Bog.* She pops up and puts the book in her pocket.

"I'll bring you down to the dining room," Belly says, and leads the way.

We arrive in a huge room with a long, shiny wooden table in

the center. It's set with gleaming gold utensils, and platters of food. Pancakes. Scrambled eggs. Toast. Little dishes of jam. Plus orange juice and fruit. Mmm. Breakfast always makes me feel better. Especially pancakes.

Minerva and Lawrence enter the room. Minerva is wearing an elegant white dress with a green scarf tied around her neck. Lawrence has on a green suit with silver buttons. He's wearing a long silver belt — more like a sash — that's looped around his waist. The name tag on his suit lapel reads: ROYAL ADVISOR.

"Good morning, children!" Lawrence says to me and Jonah. "Join us."

Lawrence and Minerva sit down at the head and foot of the table, and Jonah and I sit in the middle, across from each other. Belly brings in a bone for Prince and he gnaws at it happily under the table.

"How did you sleep?" Minerva asks, passing trays of food to me and Jonah. She's asking both of us, but she's only looking at me.

"So well!" Jonah says, eagerly serving himself pancakes, eggs, and toast.

"And you, Abby?" Lawrence asks. "How did *you* sleep?"

"Um . . ." I hesitate as I put a scoop of scrambled eggs on my plate. I can't say that I didn't sleep at all, that I was freaked out about falling the entire night. That would be rude. "I, um, slept fine," I lie.

But I can't help the giant yawn that escapes me. Ow. My neck is still stiff. I reach up to massage it a little.

Lawrence is staring at me.

Belly is staring at me.

Minerva is staring at me.

What is with all the staring in Bog? Is it a tradition, too?

"You don't look fine," Lawrence tells me, eyes gleaming. "You look exhausted."

Again? Don't people know that it's rude to tell someone that they look tired? It's basically saying they're not looking good. I mean, I'm sure I *do* look tired. I *am* tired. Really, really tired!

"I didn't sleep well," I admit. "I wasn't that comfortable on top of all the mattresses. Sorry."

"Aha!" Lawrence cries.

Minerva is beaming.

Belly looks positively thrilled.

Jonah pauses while chewing a piece of toast. There's jam on his chin. He looks at me and raises an eyebrow.

Here I was, trying not to make them feel bad that I had the

44

worst night's sleep of my life. And now they're cheering the fact that I had the worst night's sleep of my life?

"Let me explain why we're so excited," Lawrence says.

"Please do. Because I really don't get it," I snap.

He laughs. "All right. As I mentioned, the king of Bog died just last month," Lawrence says. He touches a hand to his heart for a moment. "He never married or had any children," he continues. "So there is no heir to take over as king or queen of Bog."

"That's terrible," I say. "He didn't have a will?" I know all about wills. Estate law is one of the important parts of law. I don't think I'm going to be an estate lawyer — it sounds a little boring. But I will definitely have to study it when I go to law school.

"He did leave a will," Lawrence says, sipping his coffee. "Before the king died, he decreed that the next ruler should be a princess."

Jonah frowns. "Why not a prince?"

"The king once had a sister who got very sick," Minerva explains. "She would have been princess of Bog had she lived. So he wanted a new princess to serve in her honor."

I pause with my forkful of scrambled eggs midway to my

mouth. "But how can there be a princess if the king didn't have a daughter?" I ask.

"Good question," Lawrence says. "It's been my job to find a princess. According to Bog tradition, she must be between the ages of eight and fifteen. The problem is that there are no princesses in any of the neighboring kingdoms. And the one distant heir who might have agreed to rule Bog didn't like the hot and humid weather and left just minutes after her arrival. So we have to find someone."

"Wow," Jonah says. "I can't imagine giving up a kingdom just because it's hot."

"Princesses are extremely delicate, young man," Lawrence explains. "In fact, here in Bog we have a princess test."

"A princess test?" I ask.

"Anyone can claim to be a princess," Lawrence says. "But there is one way to know *for sure* if someone is princess material."

He can't possibly be talking about the pea test, can he?

No. Impossible.

"How?" Jonah asks.

"By putting a pea under one hundred mattresses," Lawrence says.

Oh, wow. He is.

"Only a princess sleeping on such a bed would be delicate enough to feel the pea," Lawrence continues. "Then we know that person is destined to be the princess!"

"So of course we performed the princess pea test on all the girls in the kingdom," Minerva jumps in. "All of them! Even the staff! Even Belly! But no one passed. Not one girl could feel the pea."

"Maybe your mattresses are too comfortable," Jonah points out.

"That's not it," Minerva says. "It's that we haven't found the right girl." She pauses and looks at me. "Until now."

Uh-oh.

"Abby," Lawrence says, "how old are you?"

"I'm ten," I say, my back tingling.

"Excellent," Lawrence says, and gets to his feet. "Now, I have something important to show everyone. Please follow me."

I am starting to feel uncomfortable. They didn't . . . No. They couldn't have . . . They didn't put the pea under my mattress, did they?

"Can I bring my pancake?" Jonah asks.

Lawrence smiles. "Of course!"

We all stand and follow Lawrence up the stairs — me, Jonah, Minerva, Belly, and Prince.

He's not taking us to our room, is he?

He takes us to our room.

He's not going to point to my bed, is he?

He points to my bed.

"Abby," Lawrence declares, "when you showed up out of the blue last night, seeking shelter from the storm, Minerva and I decided to test you! And you couldn't sleep! Because you felt the pea!"

"What pea?" Jonah asks.

"The one under the very bottom mattress," Minerva says. "I asked Belly to put it there while she was making up your bed last night."

"Belly, be a dear and go up to the top and remove the mattresses one by one," Lawrence says.

This could take a while.

Belly climbs up the ladder. She pushes the top mattress off. Minerva moves that mattress against the wall. Then Belly tosses off the next mattress. Then the next and the next and the next.

A half hour later, only one mattress remains.

Lawrence lifts up the last mattress. "There!"

"What?" I ask, peering over.

"See that?" he asks.

"I don't see anything," Jonah says.

Prince sniffs. He lunges.

"No, Prince!" I say, holding him back.

Because I see it. I see the pea!

It's smushed. But there it is. Right in the center of the bottom of the mattress. It's green and tiny.

I felt that? Under a hundred mattresses? That's why I had so much trouble sleeping?

No way. I had trouble sleeping because I was fifty feet in the air.

"Can Prince eat the pea?" Jonah asks.

"Sure, why not?" Lawrence says. "After all, he's a royal dog!"

"A royal dog?" I repeat, looking from Lawrence to Minerva to Belly.

"Yes! Hurrah!" Lawrence cheers. "You, Abby, are the princess we have been waiting for! You will rule the kingdom of Bog!"

Me?

Princess?

Oh, wow.

I really, really messed up the story this time.

chapter six

Fit for a Princess

Jonah bows. "Princess Abby, I'm proud to be your brother."

"Jonah, it's not funny." I turn to the others. "Guys. I hate to disappoint you. But I am not a princess."

"Of course you are!" Minerva cries. "You felt the pea!"

I turn to look at the pea again, but Prince has already swallowed it in one happy gulp.

"Jonah," I say to my brother, "tell them I'm not a princess."

"Well, you're not *not* princess material," Jonah says, eating his pancakes off the plate he carried into the room. "You're definitely bossy. You love telling people what to do."

"You're not helping!" I say.

"Your first order of business," Lawrence says, ignoring my argument with Jonah, "will be to oversee your royal welcome ball. Oh, how the villagers will love a big party at the castle! We'll have it tonight!"

I can't be their princess! I'm in fifth grade and have a book report due Monday! I can't run a kingdom — I can barely do my own laundry!

"I'm not a princess!" I insist.

"You are now," Lawrence says. "You passed the test."

"It'll be my pleasure to serve you, m'lady," Belly says, bowing before me.

Oh, brother.

"I'm really sorry," I say. "But I can't possibly be the princess of Bog. I have to get home in two days!"

"You can't say no," Lawrence says. "We need you."

"Bog desperately needs a leader," Minerva seconds.

"How about if you try it out?" Lawrence offers. "For at least one day. See what you think. Please. We beg of you. We Bog beg of you."

I look at Jonah. He grins and bows again.

I sigh.

"Well, what does the princess need to do besides plan her royal ball?" I ask. Maybe by the time I have to leave, a new princess — the REAL princess of the story — will turn up. And her welcome ball will be all planned for her. I mean, she has to turn up sometime soon. It's *The Princess and the Pea*! The princess! It's HER story!

"You'll sit on a padded throne while maids fan you with palm fronds and bring you snacks of your choice," Lawrence says. "While you make decisions about hors d'oeuvres for the party, maids will gently rub your temples to ward off too much hard thinking."

Hmm. That sounds kind of relaxing.

"Well . . ." I guess it couldn't hurt. It's not like I'm in a rush. I have two more days here.

Besides, back home, I'm not good enough to be leader of the carnival. Here, I'm a princess!

A royal princess with my very own kingdom.

Take that, Anisa. Have fun with your pink and blue cotton candy while I run a KINGDOM!

I turn to Lawrence and Minerva. "Princess Abby at your service," I say.

* * *

I've been the princess of Bog for two hours and IT'S THE BEST THING EVER.

Belly gave me an amazing shoulder massage and foot rub with lotion that smelled like vanilla and lemon.

My hair, which was crazy curly because of the humidity, is now in sleek ringlets and coiled on the top of my head in a bun. The Bog crown, made of bamboo and leaves and dotted with green jewels, is atop my head.

Yes, I say *atop* now. As royal people do.

I also say *quite*. As in, I am quite relaxed.

I follow Minerva down the grand hallway, wearing the green velvet bathrobe they gave me.

"Now it's time for you to pick out your dresses," Minerva says. "As wife of the royal advisor, I wear many fancy dresses and gowns, so I'm happy to help you choose."

"Dresses? I need more than one?" I ask.

Minerva nods solemnly. "You'll need one for dinner, one for the evening activity, one for breakfast, another for lunch, another for dinner, and so on. I think you should choose twenty-five to be safe."

Twenty-five dresses? That's a lot of dresses. I don't think I even have that many pairs of underwear. In fact, I'm sure I don't.

Minerva stops in front of a pink-and-gold doorway.

"This is your new room," Minerva says, ushering me inside.

There are a hundred mattresses piled on top of one another.

"Minerva?" I say. "As princess, I can sleep on only ONE mattress, right?"

"Well, of course, but here in Bog, we are mattress specialists! Without that pea, you'll sleep like a baby from now on. Best mattresses of any kingdom, hands down. And you can sleep on one hundred of them!"

I lift my finger. "I really just want to sleep on one. One amazing, comfortable, Bog-made mattress."

"Anything for our new princess," Minerva says. "Belly! Come remove ninety-nine of the mattresses, please!"

Belly rushes in. "Of course."

"Just give Belly a list of your demands," Minerva instructs.

Oh. I feel bad telling Belly what to do. "Really?" I ask. "I don't want to put you out."

"You're not putting her out," Minerva says. "It's her job!"

Belly climbs the ladder and begins removing the ninety-nine stacked mattresses.

Meanwhile, Minerva walks over to an enormous wardrobe and opens it. There are at least a hundred dresses inside. Wow. Also rows of shoes and jewelry boxes.

"Pick your favorites!" Minerva says with a smile. "Whatever you like is yours."

I could get used to this.

I pick dresses. I pick shoes. I pick jewelry. So pretty. So sparkly.

Another maid, who is at least six feet tall, appears in the doorway. "Princess Abby, I've come for your snack order," she says.

"Anything you desire," Minerva adds.

I think for a second, then decide. "Can I have an ice cream float with double chocolate-chip ice cream and whipped cream and a cherry? No, two cherries. Three!"

"Of course," the maid says.

"Can I have one, too?" Jonah asks, poking his head in the door. "Whoa. What happened to your hair, Abby?"

"I got it done," I say, glancing in the mirror. "Do you like it?"

"You look like you're about to enter a Miss America pageant."

"Is that good or bad?" I ask.

"I'm not sure."

"Where's your room?" I ask Jonah. He's wearing fancy blue pants of a very soft material, and a white button-down shirt. He looks quite royal, too.

"Just down the hall," he says. "I still have a hundred mattresses! And did you see Prince?"

"No. Where is he?"

"Prince!" Jonah calls out.

Prince scurries into my room. He now has a Bog collar made of bamboo and leaves, dotted with jewels like my crown. He's been bathed and fluffed, and he smells like soap.

Ruff! Ruff! he barks as I lean over and scratch behind his ears. I guess we're all getting used to this new royal lifestyle.

I yawn and try to cover it with my hand.

"You must be exhausted after your terrible night's sleep on that horrible pea," Minerva exclaims. "Belly, is her bed ready?"

"It is!" she says. "One mattress left!"

"Is it fluffed?"

Belly fluffs the pillow and turns down the blanket.

"In you go," Minerva says.

I slide into the cool sheets. Ahhh.

"Why don't we let the princess sleep," Minerva says to Belly, Jonah, Prince, and the super-tall maid who was taking our snack order.

The tall maid nods. "Your Highness, we shall have your ice cream sundae waiting for you after your nap."

Your Highness! Ha!

I could get used to this, I think, as I fall asleep smiling.

chapter seven

Having a Ball

After my royal nap and my royal ice cream sundae, I'm in my royal office on my royal desk chair with a padded blue royal cushion.

"Which type of smoothie would you prefer to be served at the ball?" Minerva asks me. "Blueberry or strawberry?" She hands me a taster of each.

I drink one. And then the other.

"I'm not sure," I say. "They're both delicious. Can we offer both?"

"Absolutely," she says, writing something in her notepad.

There's a knock on the door.

I spin around on the chair. Whee! "Come in," I call.

Belly enters with a tray. "Your brother said you like bagels, smoked salmon, and cream cheese, so I thought you might like that for a snack. And some chocolate milk."

"Yay!" I say. "All this ball planning makes a princess hungry. Thanks, Belly."

She curtsies and dashes out.

How I wish I could invite my friends — and Penny — to the ball. I would LOVE to see Penny curtsy and bow before me. Ha!

According to Minerva, we'll be inviting royals from the closest kingdoms: Bug, Oceania, and Lagoon. The king and queen of Bug have one son — Prince Micha, whom Belly told us about. The widowed queen of Oceania has triplet baby boy princes. And the king and queen of Lagoon have two young boys as well. No princesses to be found.

So where did the princess in the actual fairy tale come from? In the story, she just shows up in the rain. But in this story, the only girl who showed up in the rain . . . is me! Am *I* the REAL princess? No. I can't be!

Minerva also sent a bunch of invitations out to the villagers. Everyone is coming.

The party is going to be AMAZING. Definitely better than a school carnival.

There's another knock on the door. "Come in," I call.

Jonah bursts in with Prince. "Abby! You have to come explore!"

"But I love sitting on my desk chair," I say. "It's like a throne! Bagel crumb?" I ask, pointing at the plate.

"Gee, thanks," Jonah says, rolling his eyes. "But Belly made me a tuna melt. She gave me a tour of the castle, too. She showed me a secret passageway!"

Prince looks at the crumbs longingly, and I let him have them.

"Now that I have you both in one room," Minerva says to me and Jonah, "it's time for you to practice your royal waves."

"Okay," I say.

Minerva shows us how to hold up our right hands. "Excellent. Now cup your hand," she says, "and move it gently back and forth several times." She demonstrates.

Jonah copies, exaggerating the move. I have to laugh.

I practice walking up and down the carpet in my office, giving the royal wave. "Hello, my subjects," I say, lifting my chin.

"Fantastic," Minerva says. "You're a natural."

I nod. I quite believe I am.

* * *

"Announcing Her Highness," Lawrence calls later that night, "Princess Abby of Bog!"

I make my way down the grand staircase, giving the royal wave. I can barely hear a thing over the loud cheering and clapping.

I'm wearing a royal blue floaty dress with silver sandals. Belly touched up my hair and gave me a clear manicure and pedicure. She doesn't talk much, that Belly, but Minerva was busy catching me up on all the royal gossip. The Oceania triplet boys are all a bit wild. They insist on pretending to be dogs wherever they go, and their mother just lets them. The Lagoon family always dresses identically. And Prince Micha is the worst. Minerva admitted that Lawrence was so intent on finding a princess because he was worried that without a royal in charge, Micha would try to take over Bog.

"My husband needs help," Minerva admitted. "He's getting older and he's exhausted."

And now here he is announcing me. He does look tired. I see the bags under his eyes. But unlike him this morning, I'm not going to POINT THEM OUT TO HIM.

The flash of the royal camera goes off as the royal photographer captures the moment.

Jonah, in a fancy green suit, and Prince, wearing his royal collar, await me at the bottom. "Here she comes," Jonah sings. "Miss America . . ."

"Very funny," I whisper.

"Princess Abby's coronation ceremony will take place at week's end," Lawrence tells the crowd. "But she has already signed an official document making her our temporary royal ruler."

I really did. I signed it with a royal feather and royal ink and everything. But I won't actually be able to go through with the coronation part. At some point, the real princess is going to show up. And I'll go home. The right thing to do would be to stop getting everyone's hopes up and refuse to play princess.

Yeah. I should do that. For sure.

"Dog-in-a-blanket?" a waiter asks me, holding out a tray.

Jonah smiles gleefully. He instructed the waiters to name the little hot dogs that. Jonah has always said that the name pigs-in-a-blanket doesn't make any sense.

"Mini pineapple pizza, Your Highness?" another waiter offers.

"Yes, please," I say, taking one. I requested those. They're my favorite.

Maybe I can just be a princess for a little longer.

"Ruff! Ruff! Ruff!" bark the triplet Oceania boys. They are all on their hands and knees. Prince barks back at them playfully and they go even more nuts.

The Lagoon family is far more refined. The king, queen, and two princes walk through the room, nodding and smiling. They are all wearing matching red tuxedos, including the queen.

"I can't believe Bog is famous for their mattresses," I hear a guy behind me say, his voice snide. "The beds this kingdom makes are the WORST. Lumpy and uncomfortable. I would never sleep on a Bog bed. Never."

I turn around to see a boy a few years older than I am. He has blond hair to his shoulders, pale skin, green eyes, and is wearing a white-and-gold shirt tucked into preppy, white linen shorts. A silver crown is on top of his head. He's talking to a bunch of other boys, who are hanging on his every word.

As Belly passes by with a tray of blueberry smoothies, I whisper, "Who's that guy?"

She glances at him, wrinkles her nose, and whispers back, "Prince Micha of Bug."

Aha. I should have guessed!

"I mean, no wonder Bog managed to find a princess with

their dumb princess test," Prince Micha goes on. "*Anyone* would have a horrible night's sleep on a Bog-made mattress!" He throws back his head and laughs. His entourage laughs, too.

"*Exsqueeze me?*" I say to him. "I'm Princess Abby and I had a great nap on a Bog mattress. The mattresses are the best ever!"

"Best at being lumpy and giving nightmares, maybe," he says with a smirk. He grabs a smoothie from Belly's tray, downs it, and thrusts his glass back at her.

What a jerk.

"This party is a total bore, guys," Prince Micha says to his people. He reaches down to scratch a mosquito bite on his leg. "Let's go."

"Can I take your picture?" asks the royal photographer.

"Take my right side," the prince says, turning to the left. "That's my good side."

The flash goes off.

"Now let's get out of here." He scratches some more.

"We don't want you here anyway," I say.

Prince Micha narrows his eyes at me, scratches his leg again, and storms out.

Something tells me I'm already on his *bad* side.

chapter eight

Brainstorm

t he rest of the ball goes smoothly. I dance with Jonah, sample more dogs-in-a-blanket, and meet all the various members of the royal court who are in charge of important areas of the kingdom. There are a lot of people who apparently do a lot of important things. There's the minister of villagers, who's responsible for sharing the villagers' concerns with the court. The minister of food and agriculture, the minister of culture, and more. The women ministers wear silver-and-purple dresses and the men ministers wear purple suits with silver sashes around their waists. I shake a lot of hands and give a lot of royal waves. Before I know it, it's time for bed on my single mattress.

I wake up the next morning refreshed. I stretch my arms over my head and enjoy the soft touch of the cool satin sheets on my skin. Ahhh. I had the best sleep! That awful Prince Micha is so wrong about Bog's mattresses. A hundred of them is wonky, but one is just perfect.

I slide out of the bed and make my way to Jonah's room. He and Prince are staring out the window. Prince is doing his weird low growl, his ears flattened against his head.

Grr-woof! Prince barks, then lets out a whimper-whine and puts his head down. A second later, he looks out the window again and growls.

"What's bothering Prince?" I ask.

"The alligators!" Jonah says. "We saw them. They just climbed onto the bank and ran after an old man! It was crazy!"

"Yikes," I say. "Is the man okay?"

"Yeah," Jonah said. "But it was close."

"They need a better wall," I say, peering out the window. "If the alligators are getting out." I mean, it's one thing to respect the swamp creatures, but it's another to let them attack innocent people.

"They really do." Jonah smiles. "What do you have planned for today, Princess? Want to explore the castle after breakfast?"

"Absolutely," I say.

We have fresh orange juice and French toast in the dining room, and then we make our way down a hallway we haven't seen yet. The floor is marble, and watercolor paintings cover the walls. I feel a little like we're in a museum. We pass a room on our right, and I spot Royal Advisor Lawrence bent over papers at a wooden desk, deep in concentration. Aha. We found his wing!

"Hi, Lawrence," I say.

He looks up. "Princess Abby! I hope everything is to your satisfaction."

"Everything is great!" I say.

"Nothing needs adjusting?" he asks.

"Oh . . . um . . . Well, when I was looking out the window before, I noticed that some of the alligators can get over the moat wall. Maybe we can build that a little higher so the villagers don't get hurt. Jonah said he saw a man almost get attacked earlier."

Lawrence smiles and walks over to me. He pats me on the head. "Oh, my dear princess," he says. "You're so kind to worry about the villagers. But I meant, does anything in your room need adjusting? Like the temperature?"

"Oh. The temperature is fine. And I'm more worried about the villagers. Isn't that part of being princess of Bog?"

"Aren't you just the sweetest!" Lawrence says, putting on his glasses. "Don't you worry your pretty little head about such matters."

I frown. "But a higher wall would —"

"Dear," Lawrence interrupts, "I do believe that Minerva is having Belly set up the wading pool for you and your brother and Prince. Why not change into your swimsuits and take a nice swim? Wouldn't you like to take a nice swim?"

Lawrence sits back down and focuses on the paperwork in front of him again.

The man is clearly not interested in my opinions on Bog.

"Come on, Abby, let's swim!" Jonah says, pulling my arm.

"As long as it's not in the moat," I grumble.

Prince started wagging his tail at the word *swim*. Lucky he's already dressed for the water.

When we step out of Lawrence's study, Belly is waiting for us, and escorts us back to our rooms to change.

I find twelve bathing suits on my bed to choose from. One in every color, some striped, some flowery, some with ruffles. I choose a blue tankini with a matching ruffled skirt. Jonah comes into my room, wearing red swim trunks with little palm trees on them.

"Can I help you with anything before I escort you all to the pool?" Belly asks.

"All good," I say.

Once we get outside, I realize it's not quite as humid today. But then I see four maids, two on each side of the patio area, fanning enormous palm fronds at the two lounge chairs by the pool.

Their arms must totally ache.

"Um, Belly?" I say. "Since we're going swimming, those girls don't need to fan us."

Belly motions to the maids and they put their arms down. They look relieved.

I sit down on the padded lounge chair under a pink-and-purple umbrella. There's a basket of stuff on a little table. Sunblock, which I slather on, flip-flops in our sizes, sunglasses, and two floppy sun hats.

Jonah stretches out on the chair beside mine and puts on the sunblock, then chooses the aviator-style sunglasses and the big green hat. Prince laps at a bowl of water on a little mat with his name embroidered on it. The staff here sure works fast.

From our spot, we can't even see the moat or the snapping alligators.

"So, Belly," I say, "I mentioned something to Lawrence

about the kingdom — about building a higher wall around the moat so the alligators don't attack the villagers. But he kind of brushed me off."

"Ah," Belly says, biting her lip. She glances around as if she's not sure she should say anything. "Lawrence is a good person, but he's used to running the show here in Bog."

"Doesn't he want a break?" Jonah asks.

Belly peers in the window where we can see Lawrence's head bent over his papers.

"I don't think he does," Belly says. "The king was sick for a long time and was basically a figurehead, so —"

"What's a figurehead?" Jonah asks. "Like the bobbleheads I have at home?"

"Well, I'm not sure what a bobblehead is," Belly says. "But a figurehead is a person who appears to be the leader but doesn't really lead."

Jonah scrunches up his forehead. "Why wouldn't a leader want to lead? It's in the name!"

Belly laughs. "Yes. But sometimes the leader is too old. Or sick. Or sometimes, they're just not that smart. So there's someone else behind the scenes, making the decisions."

"So the king was a just a figurehead," I say. "And Lawrence was the one really doing the leading."

"Right," Belly says.

"Then why bother finding a new princess at all?" Jonah asks. "Why doesn't he just lead the kingdom himself?"

I remember what Minerva said last night. "He's afraid that if we don't find a real royal to at least look like an official leader, Prince Micha of Bug might take us over."

"Right," Belly says.

"So he's basically looking for another figurehead," I say. "Which he thinks is me."

"Exactly," Belly says. "He just wants it to look like you're running Bog. If you leave, he'll find another figurehead princess."

But that's unfair to the girl who's meant to be a *real* princess of Bog. He just wants a faux ruler who takes naps and gets her hair done and swims and parades around in her (extremely pretty!) dress collection.

But Bog needs a real ruler.

A TRUE princess.

But the real princess, the one from the story, is nowhere to be found.

So how am I going to find a princess to lead Bog?

I rest my royal head against the pillow of my lounge chair, and think. Even though, according to Lawrence, I shouldn't do such a tiring thing.

Come on, Abby. How can you find a princess in a land without princesses?

I run my fingers through one of my ringlets. My Miss America ringlets. If only we could have a Miss Bog contest to find the princess.

Oh! I sit up. Maybe we can.

chapter nine

Dial P for Princess

belly, will you call everyone into the Great Hall in half an hour?" I ask, standing up. "Lawrence, Minerva, and the whole royal court. I'd like to hold a meeting."

Belly's eyes bug out. "A meeting?" she repeats. "Shouldn't you ask Lawrence about that first?"

I shake my head. "I'm the princess of Bog. For now, anyway. So I'm calling a meeting."

Belly nods, looking impressed. As she should. I can be very impressive.

"What's your plan, Abby?" Jonah asks me, intrigued.

"You'll see!" I say.

He shrugs and jumps into the pool. Prince splashes in after him.

I go upstairs to my room and change into a dress and my Bog crown. Then I head down to the Great Hall and take a seat at the table.

A minute later, Lawrence comes rushing in, glasses askew. "What's this about a meeting?" he demands.

"Let's wait until everyone gets here," I say.

Lawrence frowns. He's definitely used to calling the shots.

Minerva comes in, eyebrows pulled together. "This is most unusual," she whispers to Lawrence.

"Tell me about it," he whispers back with a scowl.

"Let's give her a chance," Minerva says.

The maids are whispering among themselves.

Soon, all the ministers of the royal court enter the room, murmuring together. Jonah and Prince slip into the back, still wet from the pool.

"Good, everyone is here," I say, standing up. "While I have loved serving as your princess, I'm afraid I can't remain in my role. I have to leave Bog to go home. But first, I would like to help you find a new princess. The right princess. And I've been thinking. Feeling a pea under your mattress is NOT the way to tell if someone is a princess."

"Sure it is," Lawrence says. "Princesses are extremely delicate. That's why they can feel a tiny pea under one hundred mattresses."

I raise an eyebrow. "Lawrence, no offense, but that really doesn't make sense. Want to know why?"

He narrows his eyes. "Why?"

Everyone is staring at me. Waiting for my response.

I square my shoulders. "Because. You don't want a delicate princess. You want a *tough* princess. The princess of Bog should be able to have no trouble falling asleep on a pea. She should have no trouble falling asleep on an *apple*! Or a pumpkin! Or a watermelon! She should be adaptable. She should be able to sleep on anything! She should be able to sleep in a tree. Or in a rowboat in a swamp!"

Lawrence and Minerva glance at each other. The maids are whispering. The other members of the court look aghast.

"You want a princess who is strong!" I go on. "Who is smart! Not someone who sits around all day getting fanned by maids. But someone who is tough enough to protect her kingdom. You want a princess who isn't bothered by a tiny little pea."

Lawrence bangs his fist on the table. "That's ridiculous."

"It is not," I say sternly.

Jonah raises his hand. "I just want to say that I would totally want to sleep in a tree!"

I wink at him. I love how he has my back. Even though I would never let him sleep in a tree.

"If we don't use the pea test," Minerva says, "then how do we find our princess?"

Luckily, I have an answer for that. "We have a different kind of test. A contest. We'll invite all the young girls in the land to compete to see who will be the next princess. Like Miss America! But without the beauty pageant part."

"A contest to pick a princess?" Minerva says. "I've never heard of such a thing."

Jonah raises his hand again.

"Isn't it also kind of like Purim?" he asks.

"Yes!" I exclaim. "Good thinking, Jonah!"

Jonah beams. He's clearly been paying attention in Hebrew school.

"What's Purim?" Lawrence asks.

"It's a Jewish holiday that falls in the springtime," I explain. "See, in the story of Purim, the king, Achashverosh, was looking for a new queen. He got all the girls in the land to come and compete. And Esther won." There's a lot more to the story, about how Esther winds up saving the day and defeating the evil Haman.

"So what qualities was that king looking for?" Minerva asks.

"Beauty. But we're skipping that part. This is not, I repeat, not, going to be a beauty pageant."

"So what are we testing *for*?" Lawrence asks. "If we're not testing for beauty. Or extreme delicacy."

Seriously? "We're testing for being a good leader!" I cry.

My brother raises his hand again. "Oh, oh! I have a good idea! Let's say I accidentally throw a spitball at one of the girls. A real princess shouldn't freak out. Especially if it's just an accident."

I stifle a giggle. "Right. So what you mean is that a real princess doesn't rattle easily."

"Exactly!" Jonah says.

"She'd be . . ." Belly whispers so low I can't really hear her.

"What?" I say to her.

She steps forward. "Um, she'd be brave?"

"Yes!" I say, clapping my hands. "Brave! You know, Esther was brave, too. That's how she saved the day."

Lawrence doesn't look convinced. He stands with his arms crossed over his chest. "A real princess should nap twice a day and have a maid blow on her hot cocoa at bedtime so she doesn't risk burning her tongue."

"We don't want a princess who can't handle her own hot cocoa," I say. "We need her to be strong. We should test for strength."

"Well, I think a true princess would be loyal," Minerva says, raising her voice. "To her royal staff and her subjects — the people she rules."

"Agreed!" I say. "What else?"

"She should be nice," Jonah says.

"And smart!" Minerva adds.

"Kind!" the super-tall maid calls out.

"And extremely delicate!" Lawrence adds.

All eyes turn to Lawrence.

Again with the delicate?

"Um, Lawrence," I say. "With all due respect, a true princess is a leader. Leaders are not extremely delicate."

Lawrence snorts. "I've never met a princess who wasn't delicate."

"Well, I have," I say, thinking back to all the fairy tales I've visited. "I've met many. And they're awesome."

chapter ten

Poster the Town

"Psst!" I call to Minerva from the castle hallway later that day.

She's sitting in the parlor with Lawrence. His face is hidden behind the *Daily Swamp*, the Bog newspaper. Minerva stands up and hurries over.

"Yes, Princess Abby?"

"I'm going to go to the village to hang up posters advertising the contest," I say. "But I've been planning the activities, and I would love your help!"

Minerva glances at Lawrence. "Absolutely," she whispers. "Just keep your voice down. Lawrence is dozing behind the paper, and it's better to let him sleep. I think what you're doing is brilliant. You have my full support. I like you, Abby. My husband needs to learn to let go. This is the perfect plan."

Hoorah!

We go into my royal office. I sit down at my desk, get out my tablet where I wrote down my ideas, and hand it to Minerva. We read it together:

1. Intelligence Test: A princess must be brainy! A multiple-choice quiz to test for smarts.
2. Bravery Test: A princess must have courage! I'm thinking something involving . . . wait for it . . . alligators!
3. Interviews: A princess must be eloquent! She will answer some tough questions in front of the court and her subjects.

Minerva smiles at me. "Princess Abby, your ideas are great!"

I beam. "Thank you." If only Principal Braun thought the same thing. "I have some questions for you, though. It would be great to have some experts to help us. For example, for the bravery test, I think we need someone with alligator experience to lead it. Do you know anyone who could keep the contestants safe and the gators at bay if need be?"

"Oh, indeed," Minerva says. "General Glover commands Bog's army. I'm sure he'd be happy to help out."

"Thanks," I say. "And are there any experts to put together the quiz?"

Minerva nods. "When you head into the village to hang up the posters, you should look for Ms. Jingle — she's a teacher at Bog Public School. She can help you with creating the exam. Oh, and I have another idea if you're open to hearing one."

"Sure," I say. A leader should be open to all ideas.

"You could add a kindness test," Minerva suggests. "A challenge of some sort. I'm not sure what that would be, though."

"Definitely," I say. "I'll think of something."

How are Jonah and I supposed to cross the bridge to go into town if Prince won't budge past the castle's front door? He keeps whimpering and looking over the bridge into the moat.

"Prince, it's okay," I assure him. "I had security make sure there are no alligators in the area right now. See?" I say, stepping close to the moat and looking over the bridge. "No swamp creatures!"

Prince tilts his head and peers into the water. No gators. His tail starts wagging and off we go.

The castle crew was not eager to let us go off on our own. First, Lawrence wanted to send us with security. Then he said we'd need maids to carry chairs and fan us in case we got tired or hot.

I told him that they were missing the point: that princesses — even temporary ones like me — are not delicate!

I insisted we'd be fine.

"Unheard of for a princess!" Lawrence said with his usual frown.

Minerva came to my defense, though. "If the contest is for a different kind of princess," she said, "then perhaps it's a good thing to see Princess Abby modeling the behavior she seeks."

Minerva is the best.

I wore the most casual dress in my closet. It's like a long, light blue polo shirt with a collar. I traded the silver and jeweled slippers for white slip-on sneakers. I think I still look reasonably princessy, but I figured I should be comfortable walking around Bog for a couple of hours in the heat.

Jonah is wearing a new pair of shorts and his old T-shirt, which someone seems to have washed and ironed.

We reach the center of the village, where there are little shops made of stucco. I count three mattress shops. About a mile away, I can see the big factory with a sign that reads: BOG MATTRESS FACTORY. The building is made of stucco, too. Down pebbly paths in every direction are small houses made of bamboo, with palm trees out front.

People are walking around, going into the stores, and having picnics on the town green. Many of them are holding smaller palm fronds and fanning themselves.

"Abby, look," Jonah says. "There's a bulletin board by the shops. Let's post our flyers on it."

"Good idea," I say. As we head toward the bulletin board, we pass a building with a purple flagpole and a sign that says: BPS. "I wonder what that is," I say.

"Bog Public School!" Jonah says. "Look, I see desks and chairs inside."

That's the school Minerva mentioned. Maybe Ms. Jingle is still there. I look in the window but don't see anyone. "It's almost evening, but let's see if the teacher is still inside."

We head up the stone steps and gingerly open the door. "Hello?" I call. "Is anyone here?"

"Over here," a woman's voice says.

I enter a classroom where a woman wearing a white dress is sitting at a big wooden desk. She has a name tag that reads: MS. JINGLE, TEACHER. Yes! It's her!

"Hello. Ms. Jingle?" I ask, walking in. "Sorry to interrupt you, but I was wondering if you could help us. We're holding a contest to find the next princess of Bog. The leader must be smart, strong, kind, and brave." I hand her one of our many flyers and she reads it. "By any chance, would you be able to put together an IQ test for us?"

Her eyes light up. "Hello, Princess Abby! I would love to help. What a great way to find a princess. Tell you what — you two go hand out your flyers and then come back here. I'll have the test all ready for you."

"Awesome — thanks," I say. "Uh, can I ask one more big favor?"

"Of course," she says.

"Can you grade the tests, too?" I ask hopefully.

Ms. Jingle nods. "I'd be honored to."

Jonah gives her a thumbs-up.

"A-plus," I say.

We leave the school and head for the bulletin board.

As we post a flyer, a woman holding a little boy's hand reads it over our shoulders.

She curtseys and her face brightens. "I have a twelve-year-old daughter!" she says. "I'm rushing home to tell her about the contest right now."

"Great!" I say. "See you tomorrow!"

A crowd of people gather around us. They all curtsey and bow and bombard us with questions about the contest.

"Are they really going to pick someone from the village?" a man asks.

"Yup. And anyone between eight and fifteen can enter. The contest is tomorrow," I explain.

A girl steps forward from the crowd. "I'm fourteen," she says.

She's tall and has bright blue eyes and long black hair that is tied in a braid down her back. She's wearing a burlap-type dress belted at the waist over biker shorts and sneakers like mine. She's holding two massive buckets of water.

The girl looks at the flyer. "Strength? I've got that!" she says.

No kidding. Those buckets are seriously heavy.

"Leadership skills?" she reads. "I tutor the village kids who

85

need extra help in math *and* rowing *and* bamboo braiding. Bravery? Kindness? Loyalty? That's me! I'm going to enter!"

I smile at her. Total princess material! "Awesome!" I say. "What's your name?"

"I'm Wendy," the girl says, shifting one of the buckets to her other arm. "How will you decide who wins?"

Luckily, I have a plan. "Those who enter the contest will compete against each other. The winner of each round will move on to the next. By day's end, there will only be one girl left. That girl will be named princess of Bog!" For inspiration, I add, "And it just might be you!"

It really might. This girl is strong, seems smart, and speaks up. Plus, she looks a little like Wonder Woman. Minus the costume.

"Hahahaha!" Someone is laughing loudly. And obnoxiously.

I turn around. Oh, no. It's Prince Micha. He's wearing his usual white shirt tucked into shorts, and his silver crown. Behind him are at least ten members of his court, all guys with puffed-out chests and smirks on their faces.

Micha plucks the flyer out of a village boy's hand. "A contest for a princess?" Micha says. "Hahahaha!" He throws his head back and keeps laughing.

My back stiffens. "What's so funny?"

The crowd starts smiling and whispering. Some girls are fanning themselves. Okay, fine. Prince Micha is pretty cute, I'll give him that. But his personality is terrible.

"Bog must be truly desperate," Prince Micha says. "A contest for a leader is absurd."

Grr-woof! Prince bark-growls at him.

"It is not," I say. "I'm guessing your position was just handed to you on a silver platter? Isn't that more absurd?"

"I deserve my position," Micha says, narrowing his eyes. "I was born a prince. Unlike you. You just passed a dumb pea test!"

I flush. "Yes, I did. But now we're having a contest. To find a TRUE princess."

"Will everyone be taking naps, then, on Bog's awful, lumpy mattresses?" He glances toward the factory and scowls. Then he looks back at me and laughs again.

I grit my teeth. How dare he! And what is he even doing in Bog if he hates it here so much?

He hops back on his horse and takes off. His entourage follows behind.

Not exactly Prince Charming.

chapter eleven

Another Knock at the Door

more rain!" Jonah says, looking out the window of the dining room. We just finished dinner. Lawrence and Minerva have already gone to bed, and the maids are tidying up in the kitchen.

It had better not rain tomorrow for the contest. I have three rounds planned. And rain would ruin everything.

Tap. Tap-tap.

"Abby, do you hear that?" Jonah asks.

I listen closely. *Tap-tap. Tap-tap-tap.*

"Sounds like someone is knocking at the front door," I say. Or tapping, really. "Should we ask Belly to get it?"

"Nah, let's see who it is!" Jonah says, jumping to his feet. He jogs out of the dining room, Prince running behind him. I follow them.

There is another series of taps. Yep, they're definitely coming from the front door. Jonah pulls it open.

A soaking wet teenage girl is standing there. Her long blond hair is plastered to her cheeks and thin shoulders.

"Hello," she says. "I got caught in the rain. Can I please come in?"

"Of course," I say. I pull the door wide open and she steps inside. "Are you here about the contest? It doesn't start until tomorrow." I guess being early shows initiative.

She looks at me, confused. "Contest?" she says.

Minerva, Lawrence, and Belly appear in the hallway.

"What's going on?" Minerva asks.

"This girl came to the door soaking wet," I explain. "She got caught in the rain."

"It ruined my hair. I just had it straightened, too," the girl says.

Lawrence lights up. "Welcome, dear," he says to her.

Minerva whispers something to Belly, who nods and rushes off.

"I'm Abby and this is my brother, Jonah," I tell the girl. "That's our dog, Prince." I point to Prince, who's sitting in the corner.

"I'm Tulip," she says.

"What a beautiful name," Lawrence says. He's still smiling. In fact, he's practically beaming.

Wait. A. Minute.

Could *this* be the girl from the story? The one who was supposed to knock on the door and is so delicate that she feels the pea?

"Do you live in Bog?" Lawrence asks. "I tend to know every villager, and you don't look at all familiar."

Tulip shakes her head. "Nope. I'm a princess by birth, from the kingdom of Marsh. But my elder half sister took over the kingdom, and she's kind of mean. So I've been wandering for days, trying to find a place to call home. I stopped in Bug but got bitten by so many mosquitoes I didn't even bother going to the castle there."

She's claiming to be a princess? This *has* to be the girl from the original story!

"So you don't have a kingdom anymore?" Jonah asks.

Tulip shakes her head.

Lawrence's face is still all lit up. "A princess in need of a kingdom?" he says. "Excuse us for a moment, won't you?" he says to Tulip. He turns to me. "Abby, a word, if I may?"

As Minerva chats with Tulip, Jonah and I go stand with Lawrence in the corner. Lawrence looks thrilled. Honestly, he hasn't looked this happy since I showed up. He's practically dancing.

"Tulip must be given the pea test," he whispers. "She is a real princess by royal birth. Surely she'll feel the pea."

"But Prince ate the smushed pea," Jonah points out.

I shake my head. "Lawrence, we've decided that the ability to feel a pea under a hundred mattresses is NOT the true test of a princess. Remember? We decided that the princess of Bog has to be a strong leader — not a delicate flower."

"But her name is Tulip!" Lawrence says, exasperated. "She *is* a flower! It is meant to be!"

I sigh. "I'd like to confer with my brother."

Lawrence scowls but moves away to give me and Jonah some privacy.

"Who do you think that girl is?" Jonah asks me.

"She's the princess from *The Princess and the Pea*! All along I've been hoping the real princess — from the story — would show up," I say. "But because she never did, I came up with the contest. But now, here she is!"

"So maybe we *should* give her the pea test," Jonah says. "And see what happens. Maybe if she feels it, she'll become princess and the story will continue the way it's supposed to."

"But . . . but . . . but maybe Maryrose sent us here to *change* the story. Maybe we're supposed to find someone to replace Tulip. I'm not sure Tulip is princess material."

"How can she not be princess material when she's a real princess?" Jonah asks.

"I mean princess material for Bog!" I say, wringing my hands. "Tulip doesn't look strong at all. I bet she couldn't do one push-up."

Lawrence stomps back over. "Princess Abby, with all due respect, you really should offer Tulip the princess test. The REAL test, not your made-up contest. Minerva, send Belly to fetch a pea from the kitchen."

"We're all out of peas," Minerva says, coming over to join us. "We didn't buy more from the market stall in the village because Princess Abby and her brother don't like peas."

"What's wrong with peas?" Lawrence asks.

"They're gross," Jonah explains.

"Have you ever tried them in mac and cheese?" Minerva asks. "They're not bad."

Just then, Belly returns, with a tray of cookies and a glass of milk, plus a fluffy white towel.

"Oh, thank you ever so much," Tulip says, drying her long golden hair with the towel. She wraps it around her shoulders. Then she accepts a glass of milk and takes a sip. "Oh, my," she says, trembling. "The milk is so cold it almost froze my lips."

Minerva whispers to Belly. Belly rushes off and returns with a cup of hot tea.

Tulip lifts the china cup to her lips and takes a sip. "Ow!" she cries. "It burned my tongue."

Tulip really IS a delicate flower. A delicate flower with delicate taste buds.

"A REAL princess," Belly whispers to herself. Her shoulders slump.

"Bog's princess will be strong and smart and brave and loyal!" I remind Belly. I lean close and whisper, "Delicate taste buds do not a true princess make!"

Tulip starts fidgeting. She wrinkles up her face. "I'm so sorry," Tulip says. "But this towel is ever so scratchy."

Oh, COME ON. I have been using those same towels this

whole time. They are not scratchy at all! They're super soft! They're like cotton balls against my skin.

"And could someone swap out the rug in this hallway for one with softer fibers?" Tulip asks. "The soles of my feet are burning."

Oh, brother.

Lawrence grins from ear to ear. "Of course, dear! Belly, bring up a softer rug at once."

"Right away, sir," Belly says, and dashes off.

Talk about picky. And delicate. She's like Penny times a million. No way can she lead a kingdom. No way!

"I think we should just give her the crown," Lawrence says to me quietly.

"Absolutely not," I say, feeling firm. "She's welcome to enter the contest along with everyone else."

Lawrence frowns.

"What is all this talk of a contest?" Tulip asks, running her fingers through her hair.

I explain about tomorrow's contest to find the next princess of Bog.

Tulip sighs. Loudly. Then she seems lost in thought for a moment and her eyes brighten. "Wait. Yes, I'd like to enter the contest."

"Are you sure?" I ask. "It's going to be hard."

She lifts her chin. "I'm sure."

Fine. She probably won't pass and then she'll have to move on. Buh-bye, Princess Petals.

Lawrence grins again. "I'm sure you'll be crowned in no time."

"I'd better get some rest," Tulip says. "I'll need all my strength for tomorrow."

"Give her Jonah's previous bed in the double room," Lawrence says. "The one with the many mattresses. And we'll see what happens."

I pull him aside. "No," I say. "Absolutely not. It proves nothing! I couldn't sleep and I am not a princess. You have to give the story a rest."

He smirks. "A rest?"

"You know what I mean. Where did the story even come from? Did you make it up?"

"No!" he scoffs. "I didn't make it up. I heard it from a reputable source!"

"Who?"

"I don't remember!"

He totally made it up.

"She is not taking the test," I say. "And that's that."

"Fine," he grumbles. "As you wish." He marches off toward his office.

"I only sleep on satin sheets," Tulip says as she follows Belly. "I hope that's not a problem. And I'll need a sleep mask, of course."

I roll my eyes.

"Abby," Jonah whispers. "Aren't you a little curious to see how Tulip would do on the pea test?"

"No!"

"Just a little?"

I hesitate. "Well . . ."

Jonah laughs. "I knew it!"

I laugh, too. "But Minerva said the kitchen is out of peas."

Jonah frowns. "True. But I have three M&M's left . . ."

"Three gross, melty, smashed, and cracked ones," I tell him. "And if you put one under a mattress, you can't eat it."

He smiles. "We'll see."

We open the door to Tulip's room. She is in the adjoining bathroom, washing up.

"Put the M&M under the bottom mattress," I whisper to Jonah.

My brother nods and darts off, slipping the M&M right under the very bottom mattress.

Meanwhile, Prince climbs up the ladder of my old bed in the room, and jumps on the top mattress.

"No, Prince," I say.

The bed starts to shake. Then I notice. There's a slight purple tinge glowing right up from the middle of the mattress.

"Jonah!" I whisper. "I think my old bed might be the portal back home!"

Jonah's eyes widen. "Awesome!"

"I'm ready to slumber now," Tulip says, coming out of the bathroom. "Can you remove your animal from my room? I'm allergic to pets."

"All pets?" Jonah asks.

"Yes," she says. "All."

Humph.

Belly steps in.

"Leave my ladder," Tulip tells her. "I don't like to feel trapped."

Belly nods and backs away.

If only I'd thought to say the same thing.

Tulip climbs up to the very top mattress, puts on her sleep mask, and lies down.

"Come on, boy," I say to Prince, then turn back to Tulip. "Tulip? Can I ask you something?"

"Yes?"

"Aren't you scared to sleep so high up?" I ask.

"Scared? Of course not. I prefer sleeping this high up. It keeps me away from any dirt on the ground. Good night."

She looks perfectly comfortable. I bet she sleeps like a baby.

Knock, knock, knock!

"Come in?" I say groggily. It's the middle of the night.

"Ugh!" Tulip says, stepping into my room. "There's something wrong with my bed! I can't get comfortable! It's almost like there's a pile of bricks underneath the mattresses."

Seriously? The princess test works?

"Why don't you try counting sheep?" I suggest.

"I don't like all that baa-ing," she says.

"How about alligators?" I ask. They're pretty silent. Silent and deadly.

"I'll try," she says. "Thanks."

She disappears.

I have to know. Is it the M&M?

I wait for Tulip to go back to her room, and then sneak down the hall after her.

"What's happening?" Jonah asks, suddenly behind me.

"Why are you up?" I ask.

"I heard Tulip. What's wrong with her?"

"She can't sleep!" I sigh. "I was going to take out the M&M and see if that actually makes a difference."

"I'll get it," he says.

"You will, won't you?"

We both know what he's planning to do with the M&M.

We sneak inside her room. Tulip is back on her top mattress. And she's counting. Out loud. "One alligator. Two alligators. Three alligators."

Jonah creeps over. He sticks his right arm under the bottom mattress. Then he pulls out the M&M and pops it into his mouth.

Ewww.

I look up at Tulip. A second ago, she was up to thirty-seven alligators and sounding really annoyed and agitated.

Suddenly, she's fast asleep.

Seriously?

Does that mean that the story is real? Is she the real princess?

And does that mean . . . that she should be the princess of Bog?

chapter twelve

Are You Smarter than a Fifth Grader?

In the morning, a bunch of girls are standing on the grass in front of the castle. My princess contestants have arrived!

And standing right in the center of them is . . . Tulip. She's wearing a yellow sundress with spiky heels that keep sinking into the ground.

I call her over. "Listen, Tulip," I say, my stomach flip-flopping. "I know you're a real princess and maybe it's only fair that you be crowned princess of Bog. I think you're supposed to be the princess, even if you're not what we're looking for."

She smiles. "No, I WANT to enter the contest. Fair and square. I want to prove something to myself."

What does she want to prove? She might pass the IQ test, but there's no way she'll pass the bravery test. And I can't really tell if she's kind or not. We'll see.

Tulip hurries back into place. Minerva is walking among the girls, taking a head count.

"Twenty-one girls!" she says.

That's SO MANY potential princesses.

One by one, Minerva registers them for the contest.

"Okay, all but one girl is the right age," Minerva says to me. I see a little girl frowning and kicking a rock.

"No fair that seven is too young," she says, making a muscle with her arm. "I'm sooo strong! And I'm the best at science in my grade!"

"Don't worry, little sis," an older girl says to her. "If I win, you can be my second-in-command."

"Really?" the girl asks, beaming. "Awesome!"

I personally wouldn't be so happy to be second-in-command, but maybe that's just me.

Belly hands me a megaphone.

"You think of everything, Belly. Thanks!" I turn to the crowd. "Okay, girls," I shout. "The first round of our contest is an IQ test!"

Wendy, the tall, strong girl we met yesterday, says, "IQ stands for 'intelligence quotient.' It basically measures how smart you are."

I pass the megaphone to Ms. Jingle, who is standing beside me.

"That's exactly right," the teacher says. "But before we begin this round, I want to make one thing clear."

Everyone continues talking.

She lifts her hand and snaps twice.

Everyone quiets down. Good trick!

"If you don't do well on this test," she says, "it doesn't mean you're not smart. It just means you don't do well on these kinds of tests. Some people are book smart. Some people are people smart. Some people are music smart. Some people are swamp smart. There are all different kinds of intelligence. But this is the best I could come up with in such a short time, and we have to narrow down our group. So good luck, everyone!"

Minerva takes the megaphone next. "Okay, girls, follow me into the castle library, where desks have been set up for you."

We all head into the castle. It's so nice and cool compared to outside. The maids stand in each corner, fanning the air with palm fronds. This place is obsessed with palm fronds.

The library is right off the Great Hall. It's a large room lined with leather-bound books. Twenty desks are set up in rows, all facing a large desk at the front where Ms. Jingle takes a seat. As each girl enters the library, she's handed a test and a pencil. Minerva gives Jonah the job of walking around with extra pencils and a sharpener, just in case.

I flip through the test as the girls sit down at their desks. Wow — it's five pages long. The first page is math and measurements. One question says: About how wide would you say Bog Swamp is? (A) Two inches wide. (B) One foot wide. (C) Fifty-two feet wide. (D) Two thousand three hundred feet wide.

I glance at the paper of a tall girl with spiky brown hair. She's circled A. Two inches wide.

Oof. Her *hand* is more than two inches wide. Her foot is more than two inches wide.

I doubt she's going to make it to the next round. I look around the room and wait for the girls to finish. Tulip is hunched over the test, counting on her fingers. I almost feel bad for her. But when she fails, Bog will get its rightful princess — a real leader.

I walk to the back of the room — and gasp.

Belly is sitting at a desk, staring in total concentration at a question. And she's on page five already!

"You're entering the contest?" I whisper to Belly. I'm shocked. She seems too quiet to be a leader.

She fills in the last answer of the test and glances up at me. "Oh, I'm not entering," she says, turning her test back to the first page. "I just took it for fun. You had one extra seat."

I tilt my head. "For fun? A five-page test?"

"I like tests," she says. "But I'm not a princess! I could never be a princess. I'm just a maid." She crumples up her test, runs to the front of the room, and throws her test in the garbage can.

"No, Belly!" I whisper, but she's already gone.

"Ugh, this test is too long," the girl sitting next to Belly's empty seat mutters. "Today is my day off! And this is boring." She draws an X on the top page of the test and gets up and follows Belly out the door.

Finally, after an hour passes, Ms. Jingle announces that time is up.

There are groans. There are cheers. The remaining girls walk up to Ms. Jingle and hand her their tests. Ms. Jingle, Minerva, and I walk the girls out into the hallway.

"If you wait here," Ms. Jingle says to the girls, "I'll let you know the names of the finalists in about fifteen minutes."

Ms. Jingle and I go back inside the library.

I stand next to Ms. Jingle while she grades the tests. To move on to the next round, a contestant must get an 85 percent or better.

I watch Ms. Jingle mark every question wrong on the first page of the first test, then the second. She doesn't bother finishing the grading since there's no way the girl scored at least an 85.

She does this several more times. Meanwhile, I look out the window and watch Prince playing outside.

"Finally!" Ms. Jingle says, taking off her reading glasses. "Ten girls are moving on to the next round!"

"Ten! That's perfect," I say.

We all go outside. Minerva, Lawrence, the maids, including Belly, and Jonah and I stand by the entrance while the contestants are gathered below. I glance at Belly. Her shoulders are slumped.

"I will now announce the names of the ten finalists for princess of Bog!" Ms. Jingle says, the stack of tests in her hand.

She reads name after name. There are lots of cheers.

"And finalist number seven is . . . Wendy Post," Ms. Jingle announces.

Yes! Wendy Wonder Woman. I knew she'd be a perfect princess for Bog. Of course she did well on the test!

"Finalist number eight is Althea McDorn," Ms. Jingle says.

"Big surprise," someone mutters. "She's the smartest girl in the whole kingdom."

"Finalist number nine is . . . Tulip," Ms. Jingle says.

What? Tulip? Really?

I glance over at her. Tulip doesn't look very happy about passing. That's weird.

"Go, Tulip!" Lawrence cheers.

"And our last finalist is," Ms. Jingle says, "Belly Armstrong!"

Gasps and whispers fill the crowd. The girls look at Belly with their mouths open.

Minerva and the maids are in total shock.

Lawrence snorts. "Oh, please. Belly's not even a contestant. Minerva said Belly didn't hand in her test. She crumpled it up and threw it in the garbage."

"But I uncrumpled it," Ms. Jingle says. "And put it on the stack with the rest of the tests."

Oh, wow. I must have missed that.

Belly tilts her head and peers at me. "Should I really be one of the finalists?"

I hesitate. She's not my number one pick. She's too quiet. But she passed the test, so I have to support her. Also she's nice.

"Yes," I say. "You passed the first round. You and just nine other girls in all the kingdom!"

Belly's face brightens. "Wow."

"Finalists!" I call out with the megaphone. "We'll be heading down to the swamp in one hour for the next challenge! Take a break, stretch your legs, and get ready!"

Jonah and I head back into the castle.

"I hope Belly wins," Jonah says.

"Belly? She didn't even want to enter," I say. "The teacher handed in her paper for her. But she did finish really fast."

"So why won't she win?"

"She's too quiet! No one will hear her!"

Jonah shrugs. "So she'll use a megaphone. You just don't want her to win because she reminds you of Anisa and you're still mad about the carnival."

I roll my eyes. "She *does* remind me of Anisa. They're both way too quiet," I say. "But it's still cool that Belly got as far as she did. Okay, moving on to our next challenges. Feats of bravery and kindness, right?"

"You really love being in charge, huh?"

I smile. "Yes, I do."

"Well, I hope Belly wins. She's good at all the stuff she has to do in the castle."

"It's her job," I remind him.

He scowls. "She's good at being good at her job, then. And a princess has to be good at her job."

"Jonah, clearly, Wendy is meant to be princess. I know, okay?"

He raises an eyebrow. "Guess we'll see."

chapter thirteen

Alligator Snack

An hour later, I'm back in front of the castle with my mega-phone, though unlike Belly, I don't really need it with ten girls. There will be two more tests, and then an interview to whit-tle down the finalists to one person.

One princess.

The finalists are all there. Tulip is examining her nails, which are sparkly pink. Is Wendy admiring her own manicure? NO. Does she even have polished nails? No. I smile.

In fact, what Wendy is doing is stretching her calf muscles. She's wearing athletic shorts and a tank top, and her hair is pulled back in a tight ponytail. And there's Belly! She's wearing a maid's uniform, but at least she has on sneakers and a sun hat.

"Go, Belly!" Jonah calls out next to me.

Although I'm pretty sure Wendy is going to win the whole thing, I'm glad Belly is taking her rightful place among the finalists. She deserves to be here. So what if she's only a maid? A maid becoming a princess is the ultimate rags-to-riches story, isn't it?

But I do feel bad for her. 'Cause she's obviously not gonna win.

"Hello, finalists!" I say.

"Go, us!" Wendy shouts, pumping her fist in the air.

The girls give one another a round of applause.

"The next challenge will be a show of courage," I announce.

Just like Minerva said, General Glover, the commander of Bog's army, was happy to help with the bravery test. Minerva, Lawrence, and I worked with him last night to prepare. I see the general marching up to the lawn in full uniform, whistle in his mouth.

"Okay, girls, down to the boats at the swamp!" General Glover shouts.

"The swamp?" Tulip repeats. "Oh, my. I don't like alligators."

"You just have to show 'em who's boss," Wendy says, cracking her knuckles.

"*They're* boss," Tulip says. "They'll take a bite out of me, and I would never take a bite out of them."

Clearly, Wendy will win the courage challenge. Right now, she's practicing karate.

General Glover leads the march to the swamp, which is just a short walk away.

He blows his whistle. Tulip frowns and covers her ears. I bet she has delicate eardrums.

"Girls!" General Glover shouts. "Each one of you will take a boat, one by one, across the swamp and then make the return trip. Do not stand up in the boat. I repeat, do not stand up in the boat. Got it?"

The girls nod. He continues: "Now, as you know, there are alligators in this swamp. Actually, there are all kinds of swamp creatures, big and small. And let me tell you, just because a swamp creature is small doesn't mean it doesn't have sharp teeth."

"Yes, sir!" the girls shout.

A blond girl is first. She's about to step into the metal rowboat when an alligator slithers toward her boat. "Ahhh!" she screams. "Alligator! I'm not getting anywhere near that thing!" She runs off.

One down, nine to go.

"Next!" General Glover shouts.

The girl with long red braids, named Holga, steps up and points at one of the gators. "I'm not afraid of you!" she calls out.

Uh, I wouldn't provoke him. But that's just me.

Holga gets in the boat. She picks up the oars. The alligator swims toward the boat.

"Beat it, gator!" she says, and rows confidently across the water. Two female army sergeants are on the other side, clapping. Holga rows back to us and hops out.

Way to go!

"Next!" Holga calls.

"Hey, only I get to say that," General Glover shouts. "Next!"

A petite girl with enviable biceps eyes the water. Now there are two alligators circling in the swamp. And a bunch of green lizards with their tongues darting out are walking around near the shoreline. "Um, I just remembered I'm supposed to be somewhere," the girl says, and runs off.

"Me too!" the next girl says.

"Chickens," I hear Wendy mutter.

Wendy is next. She marches up to the boat, completely ignoring the alligators and swamp creatures, which are more numerous now because of all the commotion. She gets in the boat.

"Oh, hi, gators. I know you want to bite me and possibly have me for lunch, but sorry — we all have to share this swamp. So I'll leave you alone if you leave me alone."

Wendy is courageous AND smart. I know she's going to win!

She makes it across and back without a hitch.

Next up is Tulip. She slowly walks to the boat. Can she even LIFT the oars in her delicate hands? She takes white gloves from her pockets and slips them on.

Seriously?

I see her look at the alligators, who are circling nearby. A toad hops right into her boat and sits on the front perch.

"Ugh!" she says. "I heard if you touch a toad, you'll turn into one!"

"Don't touch it, then!" Jonah calls out helpfully.

She rows to the other side. Slowly. I stare at my watch. Could she take any longer?

"Shoo!" she calls to the alligators when they start swimming toward her boat. "Shoo!"

Shocker that the alligators don't listen to Princess Tulip. But she does manage to turn the boat around and make it back to shore. In one piece, too.

Huh. That was unexpected.

"I'm impressed," I say to her.

She peels off her white gloves and puts them back in her pocket. "Why, thank you," she says.

Eventually, there are only two contestants left. One is Belly. The other is a mean girl named Morgana, who has been making snide comments the entire round.

Belly steps toward the boat. She doesn't say a word. She stares at the alligators. I watch her pick up the oars and row with even strokes to the shore. Uh-oh. The two alligators are chasing her boat.

"She's got this!" Jonah whispers.

"Don't get your hopes up," I say.

"You'll see," he says with a small smile.

Belly pays the alligators no attention at all. She focuses on the other side of the swamp. Her boat touches the shore, then she quickly turns it around and rows back. As she steps out, her eyes light up.

"I did it," she whispers to a tiny yellow snake on a tree branch.

"Oh, big whoop," Morgana snaps. "Watch a pro make it across and back even faster."

Belly frowns but doesn't say anything. Morgana steps into the boat and remains standing in the center of it.

"Did she not hear the 'Do not stand up in your boat' part?" Jonah asks.

Morgana sticks out her tongue at the alligators. She puts her hands to her ears and wiggles them and shakes her body. "Losers!" she calls to the swamp creatures. "You think you're sooo tough." She gives a karate chop. And that's when it happens.

She loses her balance.

And falls overboard. Right into the water.

Oh, no! That wasn't supposed to happen! The general promised me everyone would be safe . . . as long as they stayed in their boats!

Morgana is not in her boat!

"Ahhh!" Morgana screams. "Help! Help!"

Before the general can even move, Wendy races over to the shoreline and grabs Morgana's arm.

The alligators open their giant mouths. Their sharp white teeth are ENORMOUS. And they're headed for Wendy's left leg!

Morgana is frozen in place, her eyes like SAUCERS as she stares at the alligators moving straight toward her and Wendy.

Wendy quickly carries Morgana to the shore. Morgana drops to the ground, shaking and crying.

"I get a do-over!" Morgana screams. "I was almost torn apart by alligators!"

"No do-overs!" General Glover shouts even louder, and blows his whistle. "I told you not to stand up."

Morgana glares at him. "This contest stinks." She gets up, crosses her arms over her chest, and stalks off.

"Some people," Jonah whispers to Belly with a shake of his head.

I'll say.

"Oh — and I told you so," he says, beaming at me and then motioning with his chin toward Belly.

Whatever. I have other things on my mind. There are only five finalists left in the whole contest! I turn to study them.

There's Holga, with the long red braids, who's twelve. And Teara, a fourteen-year-old science whiz with a black pixie cut.

Then there's Belly. And Tulip.

And Wonder Woman herself — Wendy! She saved Morgana! I know she's going to win.

chapter fourteen

Tricks & Treats

After a lunch of turkey sandwiches, chocolate-chip cookies, and strawberry lemonade at an outdoor table set up behind the castle, it's time for the next challenge.

A secret challenge.

It's really cool.

It was totally my idea.

I'm jumping out of my sneakers. I can't wait!

"So what's the next round?" Wendy asks.

"Um, something to do with strength," I lie.

Wendy flexes her muscles.

Tulip looks at her own biceps. She doesn't appear to actually have any arm muscles.

Meanwhile, Belly is giving little bits of her sandwich to a friendly family of lizards on the grass. A papa lizard, a mama lizard, and three baby lizards.

As the maids start to take away the lunch plates, Belly jumps up to help.

"Belly, no need," I say. "You're a finalist — you're not at work."

"Oh." She blushes and sits back down.

And besides, it's time for the secret challenge. My super-awesome secret challenge.

I clear my throat. "Girls, because you all did so well in the courage challenge, I'd like to present you each with a gift."

Jonah is holding a small purple pouch. He reaches in and hands each girl a gold coin.

"Ooh!" Belly exclaims. "I've never had a gold coin before."

"Shiny!" Wendy says, examining it.

Tulip looks bored, like gold coins are no big deal to a princess. But Tulip is a princess without a kingdom or treasure or anything at all. And when she thinks no one is looking, I see her kiss the coin and put it in her pocket.

"Wow, that coin sure means a lot to Tulip," I whisper to Jonah, surprised.

"Just because she was born a princess doesn't mean she's rich," Jonah says.

What the girls DON'T know is that the coin IS their next challenge. We're going to watch very closely to see what they do with the coin they were given.

And now I have to hurry back inside for a few minutes and get ready for part two.

All of a sudden, the ground starts shaking. There's a rumble in the distance.

"What's that?" Jonah asks. Prince barks.

"Sounds like horse hooves," Belly says.

I stand up and crane my neck to see past the bushes lining the swamp. Guys on horses are headed toward us, galloping fast. The one in front has flowy blond hair and a white-and-gold shirt and a cape.

Ugh. Prince Micha of Bug.

He and his groupies ride up so fast that the chocolate-chip cookies on my plate bounce right onto the ground.

Great.

"Can we help you?" I ask Prince Micha.

The prince hops off his horse and walks over to me. "Well, well, if it isn't the Pea Princess!"

"Please don't call me that."

Jonah laughs. "It's kind of funny."

I scowl at my brother.

"What are you girls up to this fine day?" the prince asks.

He's actually right about the fine day. Instead of being a thousand degrees, it's merely five hundred. Maybe I'm just getting used to the heat and humidity. And my crazy hair.

"Just finishing up lunch and about to begin the next challenge in the contest," I say.

He throws his head back and bursts out laughing. "Hahahaha!"

His entourage also guffaws.

"You're not really going through with that nonsense?" the prince asks. "Are you?"

"It's not nonsense," Jonah says.

Prince Micha rolls his eyes. "Whatever you say, little man."

Jonah sticks out his tongue. Prince — the dog, not the jerk — lets out an angry bark.

Instead of leaving, though, Prince Micha and his group just stand there and watch the five finalists. The girls aren't doing anything all that interesting right now. Tulip has retrieved her gold coin from her pocket. She is gazing at it and smiling. Wendy is doing push-ups on a purple mat under a tree. Belly is sweeping crumbs from the table even though I keep telling her she's not a maid today. The other two — the redheaded Holga and the pixie-cut Teara — are fanning themselves with thick green leaves.

"Uh, Abby?" Belly says, walking up to me with her dustpan. "Why is the prince just standing there watching us?"

"Good question," I say. "Maybe he's really never met girls who don't sit around fanning themselves."

"Abby, no offense," Jonah says, "but that is kind of what everyone's doing right now."

Oh. Crumbs. But we're between challenges! That's why!

But Jonah's right. So why is Prince Obnoxious watching us? What does he want?

I'm about to ask him when Prince Micha and his band of followers get back on their horses and leave.

"That was weird," Wendy says.

I nod in agreement. But enough about Prince Micha — it's

time for this afternoon's real challenge. I need to head back to the castle now so I can change into my disguise.

"Be right back!" I call out. "I just have to pee!"

"Well, you are the Pea Princess!" Jonah calls out.

Now it's my turn to stick out my tongue.

Back in the castle, I quickly pull on the costume that Minerva designed for me. If Jonah doesn't recognize me, I'll know the costume is perfect.

I sneak out of my room and find Jonah and Prince in the hallway.

"Ahhh!" Jonah cries. "Where did YOU come from? What did you do with my sister?"

Prince whines. But then he takes a step closer. And closer. He sniffs my foot and starts wagging his tail.

"Aw, Prince knows it's me from my smell. But you didn't! Jonah, it's me! Abby! In disguise!"

Jonah's eyes widen. I look at myself in the full-length mirror in the hallway. I've gone from ten-year-old girl to an old crone — with a lifelike face mask of an old woman, a gray wig, a big wart on my cheek, a dirty, raggedy old brown dress, and no shoes.

"But why are you dressed like a scary old crone?" Jonah asks.

"I'm going to test the finalists on kindness," I say. "Remember the coins we gave them?"

"Yeah," Jonah says. "I'm the one who handed them out."

"Right. And now I'm going to walk up to the girls and say I haven't eaten in days and have no money for shoes. I'm going to see who cares — and who doesn't."

"Brilliant!" Jonah says.

I beam. "I totally agree."

"You come up with the best ideas, Abby," he says.

"I can't take all the credit," I say. "Minerva was the one who said we should test for kindness. I just had the idea for how."

"How did you think of it?"

"It's from *Beauty and the Beast*! Remember? The fairy turns herself into an old woman and asks for shelter!"

"Oh, right! Are we going to curse everyone who doesn't help?"

"No," I say. "We're just going to kick them out of the contest."

I sneak around the back of the castle so that I'll come from a different direction. I hunch my back and pull my raggedy hood over my head. Prince nuzzles my foot.

"Pretend you don't know me, okay, buddy?" I tell him. I can't have him betraying my identity.

I approach the table where the girls are, and disguise my voice and make it extra raspy. "Ooh, my aching back," I say, rubbing it for good measure. "Do I smell cookies? I haven't had anything to eat in days."

"Ugh, go away," Holga says to me. She scrunches up her face.

Aha! She's a meanie!

"At least she's blocking the sun," Teara says as she continues to fan herself with the big leaf.

Wow, not very nice, girls. A big F on the kindness round for you two.

"Can anyone spare a coin?" I ask. "I'm so hungry. And my feet hurt so much because I don't have any shoes."

Without any hesitation, Belly plucks her gold coin from her pocket. She stares at it. "I've never had a gold coin before. But you need this more than I do. I have a place to sleep and food to eat." Belly puts the coin in the palm of my hand with a warm smile.

I have a lump in my throat. Belly is THE BEST.

"Thank you," I say, trying to keep myself from tearing up.

Wendy stands up and walks over to me. "One coin might buy you a meal, but you won't be able to afford shoes, too," she says. "Here, take mine as well." She puts her gold coin in my hand.

AWWW!

"What a nice person you are," I croak out.

Tulip is the only one who hasn't said anything yet. I know how much she loves her gold coin.

"Beggar woman," Tulip says. "If you're going to buy shoes, you'll need a new dress to go with it. You can't possibly wear that old raggedy thing with new shoes." She looks at the gold coin in her hand, sighs, and then flips it into my palm.

I stare at Tulip in total shock. I didn't expect that. At all.

I blink back tears. I love all three of them!

I throw off the hood and take off the tattered dress. I remove my mask.

All five finalists gasp.

"Abby!" Belly says. "It's you!"

"Yup. And three of you passed the kindness test — Belly, Wendy, and Tulip. Congratulations on doing the kind thing."

"Yeah!" Wendy says, pumping her fist in the air.

"I'm not so sure I was being kind," Tulip says, cocking her head to the side. "It was more about fashion."

I laugh. Something tells me that Penny and Miss Princess-without-a-Kingdom would be great friends. "I don't know," I say. "You were still willing to help. That's kindness."

A smile curves Tulip's mouth. "I suppose."

Belly grins. "Wow, who knew that just being nice would make us winners?"

"I did," I say, tossing her gold coin back to her. I give Tulip and Wendy theirs, too.

"You tricked us," Holga snaps.

"I did," I say.

"Well, I'm not giving back my gold coin," she says.

"Me neither," says Teara.

"That's your choice," I tell them.

The two girls stomp off.

Belly, Wendy, and Tulip remain standing there.

But only one is going to be crowned winner — and princess of Bog.

At this point, I love them all.

Can they all win?

chapter fifteen

And the Answer Is . . .

few hours later, Jonah and I walk into the Great Hall. Lawrence, Minerva, and three other members of the court are seated in a row of chairs at the front of the room. Across from them is an empty seat. The room is packed with people.

The three finalists are standing on the sidelines, waiting to be called for their interview.

"Come on, Jonah," I say. "Let's find seats in the audience."

"Why aren't we judging this round?" Jonah asks. "You're the princess of Bog. You should pick the person replacing you."

"It doesn't seem fair for me to decide who'll be princess since I won't be here anyway," I point out. "Also, I've only been princess for like a day. And we have to leave in like five hours. It's already six-thirty at home."

"True," Jonah says. He leans closer to me. "Belly should win. She was the first to give up her coin. That means she's the kindest."

"We're not rating who's the kindest of the finalists," I point out.

"I'm just saying. If there's a tie, being the nicest could tip things Belly's way."

I sigh. "Belly is just too . . . low-key. But Wendy? She has it all."

Jonah crosses his arms over his chest. "Well, I think Belly does."

"No way will Belly do well on the interview part of the contest," I say. "Sorry, but it's true."

He shrugs and points at two empty seats in the second row. We hurry over and sit down. Prince curls up at Jonah's feet.

I look around. Many of the former contestants are here, and their families, too, as well as members of the court and villagers. Everyone has come to see who will be crowned princess of Bog.

I glance at my watch again. Time is tight. At least we know where the portal is.

I'll miss this place. Maybe not the humidity and my crazy hair. But I'll miss being able to make decisions and plan events like this contest.

"Attention!" Lawrence says to the crowd. "We will now begin the final round to see who will be named princess of Bog."

"We call Belly to the chair," a woman next to Lawrence says. I'm pretty sure she's the minister of villagers.

Belly bites her lip and slowly stands up. She looks nervous. She's definitely not used to this kind of thing.

As she walks over to the chair, I take stock of her. She's medium height, medium weight, medium everything — even medium-brown hair, medium length. She does have a nice smile, but she seems too nervous to smile now.

"Belly, please tell the court why you should be named princess of Bog," the minister of villagers says.

Belly doesn't respond.

A long moment passes.

"Come on, Belly," Jonah whispers. "You can do it."

I watch Belly. She's not saying anything.

C'mon, say something!

I knew it. She's just too quiet. Jonah has to accept she's not princess-of-Bog material.

But finally, Belly clears her throat.

"I believe I should be named princess of Bog because I care about our community very much," she says. "From the court to the village and everything that affects us. I know a lot about the swamps and how they work. I will stand up for every villager, and ensure that all citizens of Bog — young and old, rich or poor — thrive. And I promise to lead with courage, bravery, loyalty, and kindness. Thank you." She walks back over to the sidelines and stands next to Wendy and Tulip.

Wow. That was great. She might be quiet, but she's thoughtful. And succinct.

"Yes!" Jonah whispers next to me with a fist pump. "Go, Belly!"

"I now call Wendy to the chair," the minister of food says.

Wendy launches into a handstand and hand-walks over to the chair. She does a backflip and lands right on her butt on the seat.

So impressive! I can do a handstand, too, but for like two seconds, max.

The audience breaks into cheers and claps.

"Wendy, please tell the court why you should be named princess of Bog," the minister continues.

"Because I'm tough! I'm fearless! And I will get the job done. Yeah!" she shouts, flexing her muscles, which are mighty. "Go, Bog!" she says, and returns to the sidelines next to Belly and Tulip.

"I now call Princess Tulip to the chair," the minister of kingdoms says.

"Can a maid carry me over?" Tulip asks. "I've had a long day and my feet are killing me."

"Maid!" Minerva calls. "Carry the princess to the chair."

Everyone watches as one of the maids, not much taller or bigger than Tulip herself, picks her up and struggles to carry her over to the chair.

"Thank you, dear," Tulip says with a warm smile. "You're a peach."

"You're welcome," the maid responds, and scurries off.

"Princess Tulip," Lawrence begins. "Please tell the court why you should be named princess of Bog."

Tulip begins fanning herself with her mini-frond fan. She takes a deep breath and opens her mouth, then shuts it.

That's weird. Why isn't she answering?

Finally, Tulip clears her throat and says, "I —"

Before Tulip can say another word, the doors to the Great Hall burst open. What's going on?

At least thirty soldiers storm the room. They are all wearing white and gold.

Before we even know what's happening, they have our ten Bog soldiers surrounded.

"Take these Bog soldiers to the dungeon!" a guy in a gold mask orders his henchmen. "Use their precious ladders to bar the doors!"

Wait a minute. I know that smug, whiny voice. And I'd recognize that flowy blond hair anywhere. It's Prince Micha!

He's taking over the kingdom!

"Sneak attack!" Jonah cries. "Ahhh!"

Ahhh is right! Everyone is screaming and trying to run. Some villagers manage to escape the room.

"Round up the court, the pea princess and her brother, and the finalists for princess of Bog!" Prince Micha shouts.

Does he have to call me that?

The enemy soldiers are running right toward me. One

soldier grabs my arm. I try to jab him with my elbow but miss. Crumbs.

I see a soldier nab Jonah's arm, too. "Jonah!" I shout, straining toward my brother, but the soldier holding me has too good a grip.

More Bug soldiers grab Lawrence, Minerva, and the three ministers.

"Unhand me right now, you uncouth varmint!" Tulip demands. A tall soldier is holding her by the arm and she kicks him in the shin.

Prince Micha stares at Tulip. "Hey, wait a minute. I recognize you. You're Princess Tulip of the Marsh kingdom. Well, you're not a princess anymore. You're a prisoner! Hahahaha!"

"Why are you doing this?" I demand.

Prince Micha sneers at me. "We want your mattresses. Ours are the worst! And we need the alligators back! We're covered in mosquito bites!" He scratches his arm in a fury.

"You kicked out our alligators!" I snap. "And you said our mattresses were lumpy!"

"Well, I changed my mind! Too bad, so sad!" He glares at me and scratches his neck, then turns to his soldiers. "Take the prisoners to the moat and throw them in the old rowboat. It'll either sink or the alligators will get them. Take off the oars!"

"You can't do this!" I say, trying and failing to wriggle free from the soldier holding me.

Grr-woof! Grr-woof! Prince barks. He lunges for the soldier, but the guy grabs him and holds him tight with his free arm.

"You'd better not hurt my dog, OR ELSE!" I shout.

"Yeah!" Wendy yells. "Or you'll answer to me!" She karate chops one of the three soldiers holding her. But it's three against one and she can't escape.

"A takeover is not the way to get what you want," Belly says quietly.

Prince Micha sneers at her. "Oh, please. Of course it is."

Belly lifts her chin and looks him right in the eye. "No. A true leader brings his or her issues to a meeting with other leaders and helps work out a plan that benefits everyone."

Prince Micha laughs. "You're hilarious. Now get them to the moat!" he orders his soldiers.

Noooo!

The soldiers lead us all outside. They force us to march down the stone steps of the moat alongside the castle.

Prince starts growling at the water. Then whimpering. His ears are flattened against his head. He starts to tremble.

Which can only mean one thing.

ALLIGATORS!

I see one. And another. Swimming in the moat.

"It's an alligator family!" Jonah cries.

Plus, there's only one boat. It's long and wood and has no oars!

The soldiers push us all into the boat and untie it from the post. We're drifting toward the center of the swamp.

We're stuck. In the swamp. With hungry, annoyed alligators around us.

The portal back home is inside the castle. On the top mattress in Tulip's room.

If we can't get out of here, we can't get home.

"Well, at least things can't get worse," Jonah says.

And then a big fat raindrop lands on my nose.

chapter sixteen

Overboard

the rain pours down. The rowboat is quickly filling up with rainwater. This is a problem.

"I hate the rain! I hate swamps! I hate alligators!" Tulip's thin shoulders are shaking.

I think she's crying. It's raining so hard I can't be sure.

Prince Micha is standing by the palace entrance. He tilts his head. "I'll make you a deal, Princess-Prisoner Tulip," he calls out through the rain. "You are of royal blood. I will free you from this captivity if you agree to marry me. I can only marry a real princess, not some fake one chosen from a dumb pea test."

Tulip stops shaking and looks over at him.

I guess she's going to do it. I get it. She doesn't want to drown. Too bad she's about to be engaged to the worst prince in the history of princes.

"I shall send a soldier to fetch you, yes?" he asks.

She opens her mouth. I completely expect her to say yes.

"Are you crazy?" Tulip snaps instead. "You're a total jerk! I would never want to marry you! I'd rather drown!"

I'd laugh if I wasn't about to actually drown.

Tulip turns back to me. "First of all, I don't even WANT to be a princess anymore. That's what I was going to explain at my interview before horrible Prince Micha burst in."

What? Who wouldn't want to be a princess? Being a princess is amazing. Trust me, I know.

"Even when I was home, I never liked being a princess," she says.

"Then why did you enter the contest to be princess of Bog?" I ask.

"To prove to myself that I WASN'T princess material," Tulip explains. "I was so sure I'd fail. But thanks to you, Abby, instead I learned I AM princess material — smart, brave, and kind. And that means I can be anything I want. I don't know what that is yet, but I know running a kingdom is not for me. I kind of want to do something more . . . fun?"

Boy, was I wrong about Tulip. Really wrong.

I hold up my hand for a high five.

She slaps me high and low.

"Yay, former Princess Tulip!" Jonah cheers loudly.

"You mean current *Prisoner* Tulip!" Prince Micha shouts, his face red with anger. "About to be dead Princess Tulip! You made the wrong decision!" he adds. "I never liked you anyway!"

One of the big alligators snaps his teeth at Prince Micha.

"You either!" Prince Micha yells at the alligator. Then he turns and disappears back inside the castle.

I watch helplessly as our boat just floats along. Between the night sky and the rain and the fog, I can barely see a thing.

The one thing I can see? The half-submerged yellow eyes of the alligators at the edges of the swamp.

Fantastic.

I hold my watch up to my face and try to make out what time it is at home. Ahhh! It's already 6:42 in the morning at Smithville. Jonah and I only have eighteen Smithville minutes — three hours here — to make it back.

I look over at Lawrence and the three ministers. They're huddled in a corner of the boat, shaking and complaining. Minerva is so busy trying to calm them down that she isn't much help to us.

Suddenly, the alligator that snapped at Prince Micha swims right toward our boat, his yellow eyes glowing in the water.

Oh, no. Oh no oh no!

I turn to Wendy, sure she has ideas. "Wendy," I say, "what should we do?"

She stares at me blankly. "I don't know. I DON'T KNOW!" she cries. "What should we do? I just can't think under these conditions!"

"HELP!" Lawrence calls. "Someone help us!"

"Um, Lawrence," I say. "There's no one to help us. The soldiers took everyone else to the dungeons."

"There's so much rain!" Belly says. "If the moat floods, they'll *drown* in the dungeon. It's always the first to fill with water!"

"We have to save ourselves," Jonah says. "And the soldiers!"

"But how?" Lawrence asks. "WE'RE TRAPPED OUTSIDE IN THE DARK IN A BOAT WITH ALLIGATORS!"

Wendy puts her head in her hands. "I don't know. I don't know. I don't know."

Hmm. Strong. Smart. But totally cracks in the face of pressure.

"I have an idea," a voice says.

Everyone quiets down. Everyone looks around.

"Who said that?" I ask.

"I did," Belly says, shoving back her plastered-to-her-face wet hair.

The court members look at Belly for one second, then turn away and start talking again. They're totally ignoring her!

"Hey!" Jonah shouts. "Belly has something to say! Give her a chance!"

"What's your idea, Belly?" I ask.

"We MUST get the boat back to the castle," Belly says. "That way, we can get on shore and make a plan to take back our kingdom."

Lawrence rolls his eyes. "But how can we row back to the castle?" he asks. "We don't have oars!"

"Someone needs to swim and pull the boat in," Jonah points out.

"That someone would get eaten in half a minute," I say.

"I guess you're not going to let it be me, then?" Jonah asks.

"Of course not," I say, pulling him close to me.

The nearby alligator opens his giant mouth to show us his huge, sharp white teeth. I shiver and give Jonah a squeeze.

"There has to be a way," Belly says. "If we put our heads together, we'll figure it out. Brainstorm, everyone! Throw out ideas!"

Everyone thinks. Everyone is getting rained on. Everyone is glancing at the alligator teeth and trembling.

It's not that easy to think right now! Wendy isn't wrong about that.

Still, I rack my brain. Very hard.

I stare at the alligator. The big greenish-brown alligator with the gold spot between his eyes and the enormous white teeth. He's right beside the boat! We could practically touch him!

Wait. A. Minute.

I either have a really good idea. Or a really bad one.

"What if . . ." I begin, then shake my head. It's too crazy.

"What?" Belly asks.

"It's kind of risky," I say. "It might not work."

"No idea is a dumb idea," Belly says. "Let's hear it!"

"Okay," I say. "Let's make the alligator useful."

Everyone stares at me.

"How?" Belly asks.

She's not looking at me like she thinks I'm nuts for even suggesting such a thing. She's waiting for my response, giving me a chance to share my thoughts. I appreciate that.

"We need the alligator to swim to the castle for us. And pull us along."

"Yes," Belly says. "That totally makes sense. So we need to anchor the boat to the gator. But with what? Any chance there is some rope in the boat? Everyone look under your feet."

We all check. Nothing.

"No rope," Lawrence murmurs. "But, oh! I have a long belt! All the male ministers do!"

The men nod, gesturing to the sashes they're all wearing around their waists.

"Fantastic!" Belly says. "Okay. So we'll make a loop out of one of the sashes and ring it around the gator. And we'll hold on to the other end of the belt while the gator swims us ashore."

"Great!" I exclaim. "Except, why will he be swimming us ashore? He doesn't strike me as particularly helpful."

"A snack," Belly says. "We're going to throw a snack ashore."

"And by a snack, do you mean one of us?" Lawrence asks.

Belly grimaces. "I'm hoping someone has some other type of snack on them? Anyone?"

"I still have two M&M's," Jonah says.

"I think they might be a little small," I say. "But good thinking. Anyone else?"

"Oh," Wendy says. "I took an extra turkey sandwich." She reaches into her pocket and pulls out something wrapped in tinfoil. "In case I got hungry. Okay, fine, I took two extra sandwiches. I need to keep up my strength. I covered them in ketchup, though. I'm a big fan of ketchup."

"I totally get that," Jonah says.

"Fantastic!" I exclaim.

"Okay, so first I will loop a sash around the alligator," Belly says. "As soon as I give you the word, Wendy, throw the sandwich all the way to shore." She pauses and blinks. "Wait. The shore is gone! There's so much rain it washed away the shore near the castle!"

Crumbs.

"But the moat is so high, it can almost reach the drawbridge," Belly continues determinedly. "Can you throw it to the drawbridge?" she asks Wendy.

"Yes!" Wendy says. "I have great aim!"

Lawrence takes off his sash and hands it to Belly, who makes some sort of fancy loop out of one end of the sash. Then she leans over the boat and very, very carefully shimmies the sash around the gator's neck-head, barely touching him. We're all very, very quiet.

Once the loop is right between the gator's legs and his arms, Belly manages to tighten the knot. And tightens it again.

The alligator snaps his teeth but Belly is done, and safe!

"How did you know how to do that?" I ask her.

"I was a Girl Scout," Belly says.

"Ooh, you have that here, too?" I ask, surprised.

Belly nods and turns to Wendy. "Quick! Throw the sandwich!"

Wendy pitches the sandwich all the way to the drawbridge. It lands!

The alligator lifts his head and sniffs.

"Here we go!" I say.

Except he doesn't go. He doesn't move at all.

"Lazy alligator!" Jonah says.

"Now what?" I cry as our boat fills up with even more water. We are running out of time!

The next thing I know, Prince jumps up, his paws on the rim of the boat.

Woof-grr! he barks at the alligator, baring his teeth, which are not as pointy or as big as the alligator's. *Grr-woof!*

The alligator stares Prince down, but this time, Prince doesn't whimper or slink away. Instead, he jumps into the water.

Huh?

"No, Prince, no!" I shriek.

But it's too late. Prince is swimming toward the drawbridge! And the alligator is chasing him! And we're being pulled after the alligator!

"It's working!" Tulip cries.

"Nice doggy paddle," Wendy says, impressed.

"Hurrah!" Lawrence, Minerva, and the ministers cheer.

Jonah pumps his fist in the air. "Go, Prince, go!"

I am terrified for my dog. But he's doing it. He's really doing it. What a brave dog!

Prince squirms up onto the drawbridge and runs toward the castle door.

The gator, pulling us along, steps onto the bridge and drags us up behind him.

"Run, Prince, run!" I yell, my heart thumping.

Prince runs right into the slightly ajar castle door, pushes it wide open, and bolts inside. The alligator follows right behind him, and so do we.

"Ahhhh!" we scream as we're pulled over the stone steps and into the doorway.

SMASH.

We jolt to a stop. Only the front of the boat made its way through the door.

The alligator is in the Great Hall, snapping his teeth, but since he's tied to the end of our boat, he can't get too far.

From inside the boat, the rest of us peer into the Great Hall.

I see that Prince has made his way to safety, all the way at the end of the room. In fact, he's wagging his tail, looking quite proud of himself.

The alligator is still snapping his teeth. But not at Prince. And not at us.

He has his giant mouth pointed right toward Prince Micha. And only Prince Micha. *Snap. Snap. Snap!*

Prince Micha cowers in a corner, hugging himself.

"It's almost as if the alligator remembers that Prince Micha chased away and poisoned his entire family," Lawrence says drily.

Snap, snap, snap!

"What do we do now?" Minerva asks. "We're kind of stuck."

It's true. The boat is stuck inside the doorway.

"I have a plan," Belly says.

"Quiet, everyone! Listen to Belly's plan!" I call out.

She's *really* good at planning. And leading.

Beside me in the boat, Jonah beams. He was definitely right about Belly. And I guess I *was* rooting against her because of what happened with Anisa. At least a litle bit.

"Lawrence," Belly says, "while I deal with Prince Micha, why don't you go in through the side door and free our general and the soldiers from the dungeon before they drown from the floodwater. And make sure there are no Bug soldiers hiding in the secret passageways!"

"We have secret passageways?" Lawrence asks.

"Of course!" Belly replies.

"I'll show you where they are!" Jonah cries out.

"Great," Belly says.

"Be careful," I tell Jonah.

"I will," Jonah promises me. He gets out of the boat and leads Lawrence, Minerva, and the three ministers around the side of the castle.

Belly gingerly steps out of the boat and into the castle. "Hello, Prince Micha. It seems like this alligator here really, really wants to say hello to you. Should I let him?"

"No!" the prince cries, still cowering in the corner.

"All I have to do is untie this sash. And you are a goner."

"Don't do it!" Prince Micha cries. "Please! Get that alligator away from me!"

"I propose a truce," Belly says calmly. "If you and your men leave now, and sign a paper promising to never, ever attempt to overtake us again, I will not let this alligator loose on you."

Prince Micha grimaces. Eventually, he says, "Fine. But only if you promise to help lead some alligators back into our swamplands. Not this one, obviously! Friendlier ones. My people hate me for chasing the alligators out. They're constantly itching from all their bug bites."

"You'll sign a treaty?" Belly asks, raising an eyebrow.

He hangs his head. "Yes. Whatever you want."

"Also, you'll have to admit that our mattresses are VERY comfortable," Belly adds quickly. "Publicly. We can take a picture of you pretending to sleep on one, and use it as an advertisement."

"Just use my good side." He sighs. "We want you to open a Bog mattress store in Bug, too. If that could be arranged."

Belly smiles. "That can be arranged. Princess Abby, do you agree to these terms?"

"I totally do," I say. I step out of the boat and pat her on the shoulder.

Just then, the freed Bog army comes storming in, with Lawrence, Minerva, Jonah, Prince, and all the court members behind them. Yay!

"The secret passageways are clear," Jonah says, and I give him a high five.

Belly fills Lawrence in on what was discussed with Micha.

"Well done, Belly!" Lawrence says. "Princess Abby and Prince Micha, follow me to my office!"

Snap, snap, *snap* goes the alligator. Prince Micha runs ahead of me down the hall.

Ten minutes later, the treaty is signed and stamped. When Prince Micha, Lawrence, and I return to the Great Hall, the alligator and rowboat are gone.

"Where's the gator?" I ask, worried he got loose in the castle.

Prince Micha trembles.

Minerva smiles. "He's back in the water. We used a combination of teamwork and turkey sandwiches."

"That's great," I say, relieved.

"The gator preferred the sandwiches with extra ketchup," Wendy says.

"Who wouldn't?" asks Jonah.

"The Bug soldiers helped us carry the boat out," Belly whispers to me. "They're pleased about our treaty. With their lousy mattresses and all their bug bites, they haven't had a good night's sleep in years! They're exhausted."

"Ha," I laugh.

"And it's time for *all* our Bug guests," Lawrence says firmly, glancing at Prince Micha, "to go home. And stay home."

The prince rolls his eyes. "Fine. Good-bye, Bog." He looks at me. "Good-bye, Pea Princess."

I put my hands on my hips. "I'd rather be a Pea Princess than a Jerk Prince."

"Humph," Prince Micha says. He stomps through the

150

doorway and onto the drawbridge. His soldiers follow behind. They secretly wave to us as they march out.

At least it's stopped raining. The floodwaters should go down by morning.

I close the door behind them. Deep breath. It's over.

Then I turn to Belly. "Three cheers for Belly!" I say. "We couldn't have done this without your smart planning."

"Yes!" Jonah chimes in. "Three cheers!"

"Hip, hip, hurray!" everyone calls out.

Belly blushes.

Lawrence walks up to Belly and nods at her. "Belly, I've never been so impressed with anyone in my life. Your calm, poise, intelligence, bravery, kindness, and quick thinking in the face of danger saved all our lives."

He's right. She really did save the day.

"I nominate Belly to be princess of Bog," Lawrence says. "Our true leader."

"I second the nomination!" one of the court members says.

"I third it!"

"All in favor say, 'Aye!'"

Jonah is the first to shout, "Aye!"

Everyone in the room says, "Aye." Including Wendy and Tulip.

Belly gasps. "I . . . I . . . I would be honored."

I ruffle my brother's hair. "You called it from the beginning," I tell him.

"I did," he says proudly.

"I should really listen to you more often," I say.

"You really should. At least half the time," he says with a laugh.

"I was wrong to only want a figurehead princess," Lawrence says, looking at Belly. "We need someone just like you to lead Bog. I will be honored to serve as your advisor if you decide to keep me on the court."

"As long as you cut down your hours," Minerva says. "By a lot."

"Okay, okay," he says.

"Of course, Lawrence," Belly says. She turns to Wendy. "And I would like you to be head of security."

"Awesome," Wendy says, karate chopping the air.

"And, Princess Tulip," Belly says, "would you consider serving as Bog's social director? You could organize social engagements and throw parties. It could be fun?"

"I would love that!" Tulip says, grinning. "Can I be in charge of decorating, too? The castle needs a major renovation."

"Absolutely," she says.

"Not that I'm knocking the mattresses here, but have you heard of pillow tops?" Tulip asks. "They're so comfy. I had one at home."

Home. HOME! I look at my watch. Jonah and I only have three Smithville minutes to get back home before my parents come to wake us up! If we're not there in time, our parents will FREAK.

"Jonah, we have to get to the portal," I whisper. I turn to Belly and the rest of the court. "We have to take off. But it was great meeting you all."

"Thank you for everything, Princess Abby," Belly says.

"Well, I was never *truly* a princess," I say. Then I lean over and whisper to her, "I didn't feel the pea my first night. I was just scared about sleeping that high up. That's why I was so uncomfortable."

She laughs. "You're a true princess, *Bog*-style," she says, and hugs me. "That's what counts."

I smile, take off my crown, and place it on Belly's head.

chapter seventeen

Human Ladder

U h, Abby?" Jonah says as we race into Tulip's room.

"Yeah?" I say.

Jonah frowns. "We have a little problem."

We don't have time for a problem! Even a little one! "What now?"

"See a ladder anywhere?" he asks.

I look at the stack of mattresses. No ladders.

That IS a problem. Not a little one. A hundred-mattress-high one.

Prince barks.

How can we get to the portal home if we can't climb up?

Well, Jonah can. Prince probably could. But not me.

We rush back into the hallway. Lawrence and Belly are heading to my old office with a stack of folders. Her work as princess is starting right away. Good. Wendy and Tulip are following behind them, with their own folders.

"Belly!" I call out. "The ladder is missing from Tulip's room. I know you're the princess now, but can you possibly find a ladder for us?"

Wendy frowns. "The Bug soldiers took all the ladders to use as extra security in the dungeon. It will take too long to get them now."

"Just climb up the mattresses, Abby," Jonah tells me. "You can do it. Follow me!"

We go back in the room, and Belly, Lawrence, Wendy, and Tulip follow us. I watch my brother climb all the way up the mattresses to the very top, with Prince under one arm.

Okay. My turn.

"Go, Abby!" Belly, Tulip, and Wendy cheer in unison.

I take a deep breath. I stare up at the top. I grip on to the second mattress and step onto the side of the first, then try to grab the third mattress's edge to pull myself up.

I make it to mattress eight, then slide down and land on my butt.

I glance at my watch. It's 6:58 A.M. at home! I have to do this. Fast.

I stare up at Jonah way on top of the hundred mattresses.

"Okay, there has to be another way for me to get up there," I say.

"Of course there is," Wendy says. "Teamwork. Come on, guys. Human ladder!"

They all crouch down, and the next thing I know, Tulip is on top of Belly, who's on top of Wendy.

"Just climb up and then Jonah can pull you the rest of the way," Wendy says.

"Aw," I say as I climb. "You guys are the best."

I do as they say, and then Jonah helps me up to the very top mattress.

"It worked!" I call down. "Thanks, ladies!"

"What are you doing on the mattress exactly?" Belly asks.

"It's our portal home," I explain. "Long story. But we'll miss you!"

Belly, Tulip, and Wendy wave good-bye. "Safe travels, Pea Princess!" Tulip calls.

That is really a nickname I will not miss.

"I think we have to jump," Jonah says as he starts to bounce on the mattress. Once. Twice. Three times . . .

The mattress turns purple and starts to swirl.

Here we go!

"Bye, Bog!" I call out as Jonah, Prince, and I get pulled right inside, like the mattress is made of quicksand.

We land in the basement of our house at 6:59 A.M. — with just one minute left to get upstairs, into our pj's, and act like we just woke up.

I want to stop and talk to Maryrose in the mirror. But there's no time now.

Jonah and I tiptoe upstairs to our rooms. We CANNOT let our parents hear us. We'd have SO MUCH explaining to do. And how could we possibly explain?

"It's kind of chilly," I say, rubbing my arms as we race to the second floor.

"I know!" Jonah says. "I guess you get used to the humidity after a while." He tilts his head and looks at me. "See you at breakfast, Pea Princess!"

"Don't call me that!"

He laughs.

I smile and go into my room and trade my clothes for pj's,

put my watch on my desk, and then slip into bed for ten seconds of rest.

Ah. My bed. My pea-less bed.

Ooh, wait! My jewelry box! I have the most awesome jewelry box, decorated with drawings of fairy tale characters. Every time I return from a story, the drawings change, depending on how the story ended up getting changed.

I turn the box around, looking for Belly, now the princess, if not the princess who felt the pea.

There she is!

Instead of sitting on a bed with a hundred mattresses, she's sitting on a bunk bed. It's a three-bed bunk, though. Tulip is on the top bunk. Belly is sitting on the middle one. And Wendy is on the bottom one.

The three of them are so awesome. Bog is going to be a great place to live. Hot, but still great.

I hear my parents' door opening.

Ahhhh!

I run over to the other side of the room and slide under my covers.

"Morning, Abby!" my mom says as she enters my room. "Time to get out of bed."

"Thanks, Mom," I say, sitting up.

She looks at me. Then stares at me again. "Wow."

Oh, no. What's wrong? I hesitate. "What?"

"What, exactly, did you do to your hair?" Mom asks. "It's so . . . puffy!"

Oh, right. I laugh, and get out of bed. "Just trying something new," I say.

At school that day, Frankie, Robin, and I are sitting on a bench at recess playing jacks when Penny comes over, hands on her hips.

She does not look happy.

"Do you believe that Anisa Najeed turned down my idea for the carnival?" Penny says, narrowing her eyes.

I bounce the ball on the table and scoop up three jacks, then catch the ball. "What was it?" I ask.

"I said we should have a matching contest at the carnival for the two students who are dressed most alike," Penny explains. "Robin and I would SO win that."

Penny is always trying to get Robin to match with her. Today they both have their hair in high ponytails. And they're wearing ruffly yellow shirts and white sneakers with light blue socks.

"It's a great idea," Penny continues. "I'd just have my mom take us shopping for two of everything."

I roll my eyes.

"Do you want to know what Anisa suggested instead of that?" Penny says with a frown.

"What?" Frankie asks, pushing her long dark hair behind her shoulders. She bounces the ball and tries to pick up seven jacks but misses, and the ball goes flying.

"Got it!" Robin says, grabbing the little ball with her hand before it lands in the bushes.

Frankie grins. "Thanks!"

"Hello! Is anyone even listening to me?" Penny complains.

"We're listening, we're listening," Robin says.

"Anisa said she was thinking of having a TALENT contest," Penny mutters, shaking her head. "Singing, dancing, juggling, playing an instrument, reciting a poem, putting on a skit, anything goes."

Huh. I love that. And I love that Anisa stood up to Penny.

Maybe I underestimated Anisa. I've been doing a lot of underestimating lately. First, I thought Belly was too quiet, but it turned out she was the best leader. Then I thought Tulip was too princessy, but she turned out to be kind and generous. And I thought Wendy was all brawn, when she gets scared just like the rest of us.

"A talent contest is a great idea," I say. "Everyone's good at something."

"What are YOU good at?" Penny asks, raising an eyebrow.

"I'm good at ideas," I say. "And teamwork." I bounce the ball, scoop up eight jacks, and catch the ball. "Jacks, too."

And one more thing. Admitting when I'm wrong.

I see Anisa walking over to the swings. She sits down and tries to get the swing going, but obviously, swinging is not one of her talents.

I run over. "Want a push?" I ask.

Anisa smiles. "Sure."

"So I heard you want to do a talent contest at the carnival," I say, giving her a push. "I think that's a great idea."

"Really?" she says, trying to pump her legs. She doesn't get very far.

I nod. "You know, if you're still looking for a second-in-command, I'd like to help with the carnival."

She beams. "Great! I was really hoping you'd change your mind. It's a lot of work, and I can use the help."

I push Anisa even harder, and she laughs as she soars up high in the air.

Everyone needs help. It's all about teamwork. I think about an expression I've heard my nana use: Sometimes, it takes a village. That means that when people pitch in together, great things can happen.

Sometimes, it does take a village. And I guess sometimes, it takes a kingdom.

With an alligator. And good friends.

acknowledgments

So many thank-yous to:

Aimee Friedman, the queen of all editors. Also thank you to everyone else at Scholastic: Olivia Valcarce, Lauren Donovan, Rachel Feld, Tracy van Straaten, Robin Hoffman, Melissa Schirmer, Elizabeth Parisi, Abby McAden, David Levithan, Lizette Serrano, Emily Heddleson, Sue Flynn, and everyone in the school channels and sales!

Amazing agents Laura Dail and Tamar Rydzinski! Deb Shapiro! Lauren Walters and Alyssa Stonoha!

Thank you to all my friends, family, supporters, writing buddies, and first readers:

Targia Alphonse, Tara Altebrando, Bonnie Altro, Elissa Ambrose, Robert Ambrose, Jennifer Barnes, Emily Bender, the Bilermans, Jess Braun, Jeremy Cammy, Avery Carmichael, the Dalven-Swidlers, Julia DeVillers, Elizabeth Eulberg, the Finkelstein-Mitchells, Stuart Gibbs, Alan Gratz, the Greens, Adele Griffin, Anne Heltzel, Farrin Jacobs, Emily Jenkins, Lauren Kisilevsky, Maggie Marr, the Mittlemans, Aviva Mlynowski, Larry Mlynowski,

Lauren Myracle, Melissa Senate, Courtney Sheinmel, Jennifer E. Smith, the Swidlers, Robin Wasserman, Louisa Weiss, Rachel and Terry Winter, the Wolfes, Maryrose Wood, and Sara Zarr.

Extra love and thanks to Chloe, Anabelle, and Todd.

And to my Whatever After readers: Thank you for reading my books! And remember to eat your vegetables.

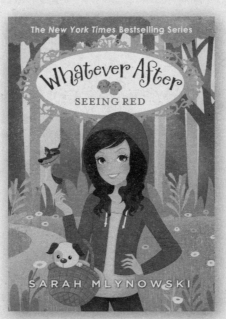

Read all the *Whatever After* books!

Whatever After #1: FAIREST of ALL

In their first adventure, Abby and Jonah wind up in the story of Snow White. But when they stop Snow from eating the poisoned apple, they realize they've messed up the whole story! Can they fix it — and still find Snow her happy ending?

Whatever After #2: IF the SHOE FITS

This time, Abby and Jonah find themselves in Cinderella's story. When Cinderella breaks her foot, the glass slipper won't fit! With a little bit of magic, quick thinking, and luck, can Abby and her brother save the day?

Whatever After #3: SINK or SWIM

Abby and Jonah are pulled into the tale of the Little Mermaid — a story with an ending that is *not* happy. So Abby and Jonah mess it up on purpose! Can they convince the mermaid to keep her tail before it's too late?

Whatever After #4: DREAM ON

Now Abby and Jonah are lost in Sleeping Beauty's story, along with Abby's friend Robin. Before they know it, Sleeping Beauty is wide awake and Robin is fast asleep. How will Abby and Jonah make things right?

Whatever After #5: BAD HAIR DAY

When Abby and Jonah fall into Rapunzel's story, they mess everything up by giving Rapunzel a haircut! Can they untangle this fairy tale disaster in time?

Whatever After #6: COLD as ICE

When their dog Prince runs through the mirror, Abby and Jonah have no choice but to follow him into the story of the Snow Queen! It's a winter wonderland . . . but the Snow Queen is rather mean, and she FREEZES Prince! Can Abby and Jonah save their dog . . . and themselves?

Whatever After #7: BEAUTY QUEEN

This time, Abby and Jonah fall into the story of *Beauty and the Beast*. When Jonah is the one taken prisoner instead of Beauty, Abby has to find a way to fix this fairy tale . . . before things get pretty ugly!

Whatever After #8: ONCE upon a FROG

When Abby and Jonah fall into the story of *The Frog Prince*, they realize the princess is so rude they don't even *want* her help! But will they be able to figure out how to turn the frog back into a prince all by themselves?

Whatever After #9: GENIE in a BOTTLE

The mirror has dropped Abby and Jonah into the story of *Aladdin*! But when things go wrong with the genie, the siblings have to escape an enchanted cave, learn to fly a magic carpet, and figure out WHAT to wish for . . . so they can help Aladdin and get back home!

Whatever After #10: SUGAR and SPICE

When Abby and Johah fall into the story of *Hansel and Gretel*, they can't wait to see the witch's cake house (yum). But they didn't count on the witch trapping them there! Can they escape and make it back to home sweet home?

Whatever After #11: TWO PEAS in a POD

When Abby lands in the story of *The Princess and the Pea*—and has trouble falling asleep on a giant stack of mattresses—everyone in the kingdom thinks SHE is the princess they've all been waiting for. Though Abby loves the royal treatment—can you say unlimited ice cream?—she and Jonah need to find a *real* princess to rule the kingdom . . . *and* find their way back home in time!

Whatever After #12: SEEING RED

My, what big trouble we're in! When Abby and Jonah fall into the story of *Little Red Riding Hood*, they're determined to save Little Red and her grandma from being eaten by the big, bad wolf. But there's quite a surprise in store when the siblings arrive at Little Red's grandma's house.

Whatever After Special edition: ABBY in WONDERLAND

In this Special Edition, Abby and three of her friends fall down a rabbit hole into *Alice's Adventures in Wonderland*! They meet the Mad Hatter, the caterpillar, and Alice herself . . . but only solving a riddle from the Cheshire Cat can help them escape the terrible Queen of Hearts. Includes magical games and an interview with the author!